# The Cowboy

# The Cowboy

## A McAllister Brothers Romance

### Julia Justiss

TULE
PUBLISHING

# Dedication

To the Justiss Family of Morris County, Texas, who have for
170 years served their God, their family and their land.

# Author's Note

Like my Navy pilot father-in-law, after retirement my Navy husband came back to buy property in Morris County, where his ancestors were among the first three settling families in the area. His grandfather, great and great-great-grandfathers farmed cotton, sorghum and sweet potatoes, planted fruit and nut trees, ran a syrup mill, operated a blacksmith shop, and dedicated their lives to improving their land and livestock. Marrying into this family, members of which still run the Justiss Ranch, inspired me to want to write a story about characters with equally deep ties to their family and their land.

Although the Texas location is slightly different—my story takes place in the Hill Country of central Texas, rather than the Piney Woods of northeast Texas—the love for the land and family is the same. I hope my McAllister Brothers stories will convey to readers that legacy of loyalty and devotion.

# Chapter One

A S DAWN SUN painted a rosy stripe along the eastern horizon, Grant McAllister kicked the banked embers of last night's campfire back to glimmering life. Patiently feeding in bits of dried grass and tinder under the crisscross tower of oak branches he'd constructed over the coals, he watched until the wood smoldered and caught, then stepped aside to fetch the grill that fit over the fire's framework. Adding water to the battered-tin coffeepot, he placed it on the grill to heat for the morning's first cup.

Once all was in readiness for coffee and the bacon and eggs he'd cook when his brother Brice arrived, he sat back on one of the wooden stumps that served as stools. With the nearest town miles away and this high ridge reached by isolated ranch roads, only the chatter of birds and the lowing of cattle in the nearby fields broke the silence. Grant closed his eyes, letting the beauty and stillness of the early June morning flood his soul.

His mind filled with images of campfires past. Many built here, on this high plateau sheltered by old-growth cedar and live oaks, where he and brothers, Duncan and Brice, had camped innumerable times while growing up. Later, in dusty bivouacs thousands of miles away, surrounded by his fellow Recon Marines, brothers in all but blood, drinking coffee made on their Jetboils, sharing tall tales and goodies from home.

It had taken a long time to reconcile himself to the anguish and loss, but after eight years in the service and two more living in a high-rise San Antonio condo, working with an organization that matched veterans with jobs, he was back in Whiskey River. The itchy feet that had compelled him to leave right after high school, carried him to various Marine bases across the US and to rocky battlefields halfway around the world, had finally led him home. To McAllister land and the Triple A ranch.

When injuries had forced him out of an active role in the Corps, working with vets had been a way to hang on to some involvement in military life. After spending two years in that role, when Duncan had asked for Grant's help, he'd decided he might at last be ready to close the book on that phase of his life.

The decision to come back felt right.

The sound of scrabbling rocks and the growl of a distant engine had him opening his eyes. Must be Brice driving up. Better get the coffee going.

By the time his brother's SUV rounded the last curve and drove across the flat plateau toward his campsite, he was pouring boiling water into the French press, filling the morning air with the rich smell of dark-roast coffee.

He heard the engine die and the slam of car doors—two car doors. Looking up in surprise, he saw his older brother, Duncan, walking toward the fire with Brice.

"Good thing you made a whole press full," Duncan said as he came over to grasp Grant's hand and give him their traditional one-armed hug. "I'm thirsty."

"What's the bridegroom doing up here?" Grant asked. "Surely Harrison hasn't thrown you out yet."

"She's up early working on the breeding books, then plans to head into town. She's been doing some tax work for Reba's Java and Mel Gardiner's bookstore, and wanted to get them the paperwork to sign before the June fifteenth deadline. So she sent me out for some 'brother bonding time.'"

Brice rolled his eyes. "Did she really call it that? Women!"

"Careful, now. That's my darling wife you're disparaging. She looked so cute saying it with that serious expression of hers; I didn't have the heart to tease her."

Grant looked at Brice and both brothers shook their heads. "Completely besotted," Grant said. "I'd call it nauseating, if Harrison weren't such a nice girl."

"Why she ever hooked up with our workaholic brother, I'll never understand, but otherwise, she's pretty smart," Brice agreed.

"Obviously I couldn't leave my beautiful bride, but why didn't you camp with Grant last night?" Duncan asked

Brice.

"If you weren't so oblivious to everything beyond your new wife, you'd remember that I had to work undercover. Didn't finish until too late to join Grant. Besides, I think he wanted a night alone to . . . to ease into being home again. You were . . . okay, weren't you?"

The anxious looks on both his brothers' faces told him they were remembering a time not so many years distant, soon after his return from his last deployment and his decision to leave the Marines, when he hadn't been okay alone, here or anywhere. Recuperating from the injuries suffered on that last patrol, dealing with the grief of losing friends—and the guilt of having survived them—had been a difficult struggle. But he'd won the battle against those demons—mostly. "I'm fine. Meditation, therapy and time—the recipe to heal all wounds. Or at least make them bearable."

"I'm just glad you're back," Duncan said, handing a cup of coffee to Brice before taking one himself. "Now that we've recovered the Scott Ranch property and restored the Triple A to its original size, I really am going to need your help. Especially after the town doc confirmed last week that Juan Cortez, whom you may remember had been helping Harrison's dad run the Scott Ranch, is barred from doing any heavy work permanently."

"Is he still in a lot of pain?" Brice asked as they settled onto log seats by the fire.

"He says he isn't, but Harrison's going to press him to see a pain management specialist in Austin. When that mama cow knocked him around, he apparently aggravated some disc problems he's had for years. With hay-cutting season upon us, I don't know what we would have done if you hadn't agreed to move back and help, Grant."

"When your big brother, who's never asked for assistance with anything, says the only wedding present he wants is for you to help him run the ranch he single-handedly rescued from bankruptcy and has worked sixty hours a week since high school to make profitable again, what else could a brother do?"

"So you gave your boss notice and hoofed it back to Whiskey River," Brice said.

"Not exactly. I'm still consulting and I'll handle a few cases. Much of the workload I've turned over to my assistant, but he knows he can call me anytime, and I'll probably go back to San Antonio once a month or so." At the startled look Duncan gave him, he added, "After I've gotten the hay on my section of the ranch cut, of course."

"Harrison and I are thrilled to have you back on any terms," Duncan affirmed. "The Triple A's been McAllister land since great-granddad settled here after the Civil War. Sure, I run it, but it belongs to all of us. It's our legacy. Shoot, maybe we'll even convince Brice to give up the law and settle back here."

"I think the two of you have it well in hand," Brice said,

stretching his legs out toward the fire.

"Too exciting chasing criminals to settle for chasing down stray calves?" Duncan said.

"Naw, he just thinks the ladies prefer a man in a tan Stetson with a ranger star on his chest," Grant said.

"Speaking of ladies, what did the one you left behind in San Antonio do when you told her you were moving to Whiskey River? Or is she planning to join you?" Brice asked.

"Meredith, in Whiskey River?" Grant laughed at the very image. "Let's just say that she has about as much love for small-town life as Duncan's old high school flame, Julie Ann. It was . . . time for that to end."

"I figured as much, since you didn't bring her to the wedding," Duncan said.

"Making commitment noises, was she, bro?" Brice asked.

"And how is that blond honey you've been seeing in Austin?" Grant flashed back. "Hankering for a diamond on her finger?"

"Okay, no more talk of women," Brice said. "Speaking of 'settling,' where do you mean to live?"

"There's plenty of room back at the ranch house," Duncan said. "You know you're welcome."

Brushing off the flake of ash that had landed on his cup, Grant said, "Sure, I'll just move in with my brother and his new wife. Or maybe not."

"If you don't want to do that, I know Harrison would be happy to have you live in the house her dad built at the Scott

Ranch."

Grant shook his head. "Too big for me. I'm used to living in a one-bedroom condo. I don't need thirty-six hundred square feet."

"Surely you don't mean to live in town," Duncan objected. "That would add on an unnecessary drive, especially in the winter when it will still be dark when morning chores begin."

"No, I have something different in mind. Remember the little hunting cabin Granddaddy built, over on the land Scott bought? Scott never used it; he built that new house closer to the center of the ranch. I rode over yesterday to look at it. Needs a new roof and some work inside, of course. Since you want me to work the cattle on the eastern side of the Triple A, I'd be right where I need to be."

Pointing off to the east, Brice said, "The cabin sits on that bluff overlooking that creek where it branches off the Pedernales, near our old favorite swimming hole, right?"

"That's the one."

"No one's done anything to it in decades," Duncan said. "Are you sure it wouldn't fall down around your ears?"

"No, the timbers and the rock walls look to be in amazingly good shape. Granddaddy knew how to build a cabin. I can clean it out, add on an extension with two bedrooms and a bathroom, and redo the kitchen. With new insulation, a gas stove insert in the fireplace, solar panels for electricity and a deck built to overlook the river, it should do me fine. I can camp out there while I work on it."

"With no electricity or running water or—?" Brice began before halting abruptly at Grant's raised eyebrow. "Never mind. Recon Marine, right? You could camp on a rock and live off dirt."

"I don't need a feather mattress and a lighted bathroom mirror so I can apply my scented hair gel," Grant said, setting down his empty cup.

"Screw you, bro."

"You can shower and wash clothes back at our place until you've got the renovations done," Duncan said. "Just to be polite, I'll make sure Harrison is okay with your taking over the cabin. Since technically, it's on the land her daddy left her."

"Which she deeded back to you, didn't she?" Brice asked.

"She's offered to, saying she wants the Triple A to be legally restored to its original size and name. I thought if it's alright with the two of you, we'd retitle the whole property, our portion and the Scott portion, with the deed in all our names."

"Are you sure, Duncan? You probably ought to own it outright, with Harrison, of course. You're the one who's held it together all these years, while I was off with the Marines and Brice was busy law-manning."

"No, Daddy always intended for it to belong to all of us. I don't think he'd mind me including Harrison."

"She's a McAllister now," Brice said. "All for one and

one for all."

"That's settled, then. Is that breakfast fixings I see, bro?" Duncan asked.

"Bacon and eggs. After we eat, I thought we'd mount up and you can drive me around, show me which fields are planted to what grasses and which ones need mowing first. I may have grown up on a ranch, but it's gotten much more scientific and specialized since Daddy had us out cutting native rye grass."

"I'll stay for breakfast, then I need to get back to Austin," Brice said.

"He means he needs to escape before we try to put *him* to work," Duncan said.

"I seem to remember that tactic," Grant agreed. "'But Daddy, I can't mow today. I have football practice.'"

"'Sorry, Daddy, but I'm supposed to run the student council meeting after school,'" Duncan chimed in.

"Careful now, big brothers. I can still whup the both of you."

"You could try, little brother, but I wouldn't advise it," Grant said. "Remember, you being the runt of the litter, we've always gone easy on you."

"Why don't you stop harassing me and cook the bacon," Brice said. "Time's a-wastin'—for getting those chores done."

"I'm starving too," Duncan admitted.

"After a night's hard work, no doubt," Grant said, and

ducked a punch from his brother before walking over to fetch the cast-iron frying pan from his kit and bacon from the cooler. "Only thing you were better at growing up than weaseling out of chores, Brice, was cleaning out the fridge of everything edible."

"An offensive lineman needs his protein."

"I'm sure. Pour me another cup, and I'll get the bacon going."

Grant took a swallow of the hot, dark brew from the cup Brice handed him and set the bacon sizzling. Listening as Duncan ragged his little brother about the mysterious Austin blonde, Grant smiled.

He hadn't been sure that moving back was a good idea, but he had to admit, it felt entirely natural to be back up here in this special place with his brothers again, their camaraderie as intact as if they'd last camped here ten days, instead of ten years ago, after his high school graduation. Listening to them hassle each other with the audacity and good humor that came from decades of affection and shared history, he felt a deep connection to them and this place.

He'd been somewhat afraid when he learned Duncan was getting married that the rapport and the closeness the brothers had always shared would be compromised. Duncan showing up this morning, his energy and good humor just as Grant remembered it, reassured him that "the three musketeers," as they'd called themselves in high school, would continue to ride together.

Although, even if it had affected their relationship, he couldn't have resented Harrison. His workaholic, serious, driven brother looked happier and more relaxed than Grant had ever seen him.

While forking the bacon onto a plate and deftly cracking eggs into the frying pan, Grant felt a niggle of envy.

Once, while he was still in the Corps, he thought he'd established the same sort of deep bond with a woman. Fortunately, he'd dragged his feet about marrying Kelsey, because her devotion hadn't lasted through the three deployments he'd pulled. Not that he blamed her—too much—for drifting away. Loving someone who periodically got called to the other side of the world for someone to shoot at didn't make for an easy relationship.

But having her walk away, and walk away right after he'd been shipped home, injured, grieving and vulnerable, needing her love and support more than he'd ever needed anything, made him skeptical of ever finding a woman who'd stand beside him through the tough times. Stand beside him with the unshakeable loyalty and support his brothers had always given him.

Much as he enjoyed the ladies, relying on family was safer. Even if sometimes his brothers did inspire him with a desire to murder.

"Eggs and bacon are up," he announced. "There's some biscuits from town and jalapeño sauce in the grub locker. Grab a plate and come help yourself."

Soon after, another round of coffee in their mugs and plates full, the brothers sat on the stump seats, watching as the sun rose gold and brilliant into the white sky. Looking around, Grant saw the peace and sense of belonging he felt mirrored in the eyes of his siblings. Of one accord, they raised their coffee mugs.

"So glad to have all of you back," Duncan said.

"You bet, brothers. All for one and one for all," Grant toasted.

# Chapter Two

A WEEK LATER, after getting up at dawn to finish the day's mowing early enough that he would have time to shower, change, and get into town before the shops closed, Grant McAllister pulled up his Chevy pickup in front of a small garage beside an equally small stucco ranch house. If it hadn't been for some assorted metal sculptures posed in the yard separating the two buildings, he would have suspected he'd taken a wrong turn when he left the state highway and headed down the narrow farm-to-market road.

He vaguely remembered this house had belonged to the manager who used to oversee the old Cameron ranch, before the heirs sold the property to one of the developers who seemed bent on covering every hilltop between Last Stand and Whiskey River with condos. Thank heavens, the valley road leading here didn't offer outstanding vistas, and it appeared few of the housing sites along it had been sold.

The ranch house looked just as he remembered from high school: small, modest, unassuming. Aside from a fresh coat of paint and a small sign over the garage announcing "Hidden Treasures," the place appeared deserted—not the bustling, upscale shop featuring unusual western-themed décor he'd been expecting.

As he stepped down from the truck, he heard a squeal of high-pitched laughter. A blond little girl darted out of the house onto the patio between the two buildings. Spotting him, she stopped short and stared.

Though not anxious for any of his own, he liked kids. But he didn't see how even a child-averse curmudgeon could fail to respond to the blond cherub gazing up at him. With her model-perfect oval face, pink cheeks, sparkling deep-blue eyes, and golden curls pulled up into two topknots, she exuded an innocent "Shirley Temple" radiance. When, inspection apparently completed, she smiled at him, he just had to smile back.

"Hello, angel. Anyone in the shop?"

"My mommy is. Jillee said I could go get her. It's time to stop working."

"How about we get her together?"

She must have been properly warned not to associate with strangers, for she hesitated. Then, apparently deciding that with someone in the house watching and her mama in the shop, it was probably safe to agree, she nodded. "Okay. I'll show you."

Remaining a non-threatening distance behind, he followed her to the garage and through the door into the shop. And then stopped short himself. Eyes riveted on the woman within, he hardly heard the little girl announcing, "Mommy, there's a man to see you."

Perched atop a ladder was a tall, slender blonde in old faded jeans, her tank top showing mouth-watering curves under a loose, open chambray work shirt. She had her arms raised above her head as she attached a lighting fixture to the ceiling.

At her daughter's words, she looked over at them. Grant felt a spark of pure physical attraction energize his body.

Her face was an oval as perfect as her daughter's, her eyes the same shade of startlingly deep blue, her mouth lush and kissable. She gazed at him, brushing back over her shoulder a long mane of pale blond hair caught in a loose ponytail, her inquiring expression as innocent and guileless as the child's.

Seeing that Madonna face in that siren's body only intensified his first, immediate sensual response.

Grant was suddenly gladder than ever he'd come back to Whiskey River.

Perhaps she, too, felt the spark between them. Surprise replacing her look of inquiry, she leaned toward him—and wobbled on the ladder. Grant was about to run over to catch her when she recovered her balance.

"Can I help you?"

*Could you ever.* Swallowing to moisten his suddenly dry throat, Grant said, "I hope so. I'm looking for some things for the cabin I'm renovating. Lighting, furniture, décor pieces. I was told you had some unusual and interesting ones."

She nodded. "I was about to close, but since you've driven all the way out here, please take your time and look around."

As she started to descend the ladder, Grant hurried over to steady it.

"Shouldn't climb on a ladder without someone to spot you, you know. Especially if you're working above your head."

"Are you from OHSA?" she asked wryly. "Please tell me you're not going to write me up for an infraction. Since I'm the owner, you can't say I was endangering an employee."

"I hope to support you. Your business, I mean." What was wrong with his brain? Okay, she was a stunner. And he did like willowy blondes. A whole lot.

But this was Whiskey River, not San Antonio. The gossip mill here worked overtime. Though he'd more or less decided to put his love life on hold while he settled back in at home, one look at this lady, followed by a quick glance to confirm her left hand was ringless, had him throwing that resolve out the window.

But if he did pursue her, he'd have to step carefully. He didn't want to become the town's major subject of discussion before he'd been back barely a month.

"Mommy, Jillee said I could come get you." The child came over to hug her mother. "She has lemonade ready. I helped make it!"

The blonde kissed her daughter on the top of her head.

"That will make it even sweeter, Katie-girl."

Turning to Grant, the child said, "Would you like some lemonade too?"

"Thanks, but I wouldn't want to impose. It's nice of you to ask, though."

"Mommy says it's good to share."

"Your mommy'd be right about that. Most of the time."

"Why don't you look around and let me know if any-thing catches your eye?" the owner said. "I'll be on the terrace with the lemonade."

Something certainly had caught his eye. So much so he hadn't paid any attention to the items in the shop. He'd inspect them after this entrancing woman and her little girl walked out.

"I'll make sure to keep an extra glass, if you change your mind. You deserve a reward for driving all the way out here so late on a hot June afternoon. I'm Abby Rogers, by the way, and this is my daughter, Katie," she added, coming over and holding out her hand. "Welcome to Hidden Treasures."

"Grant McAllister. Pleased to meet you, Abby, and you, too, Katie." The firm handshake she offered didn't mask the tingle of electricity that shot up his arm when his fingers gripped hers.

Her eyes widened. For a moment, they both stood mo-tionless, just gazing at each other. Then Abby pulled her hand away. "Come on, Katie. Give a holler if you need anything, Grant."

"Don't I get to shake hands too?" Katie asked.

"Maybe later," Abby said, shepherding her daughter toward the door. "Let's let Mr. McAllister look around first."

It appeared he'd found a lot more than potential furnishings for his cabin here. Now he wished he'd paid more attention when Harrison had told him about the shop. Had she mentioned whether the owner had a husband or boyfriend? Just because the lovely blonde didn't wear a wedding ring didn't mean she was free and available.

There was a Rogers clan that lived in the Barrels area of downtown Whiskey River; he'd gone to high school with several of them. But not this woman—he would definitely have remembered her. Since she had that charming daughter, Rogers might be her married name, though. If so, was she still married?

He might not be interested in anything long-term, but since ending his liaison with Meredith, he'd missed feminine companionship as well as the physical intimacy. If this luscious blonde were unattached and amenable to masculine company, he'd be more than happy to oblige.

*Abby Rogers, I hope to soon get much better acquainted with you.*

AFTER GRANT WATCHED the mom and daughter settle in a pair of patio chairs under an awning that blocked the afternoon sun, he finally turned to inspect the articles in the shop. Harrison had told him the owner had an artist's eye she used to transform and repurpose used, abandoned and derelict items into unusual and interesting furniture, light fixtures and decorative objects.

The chandelier she'd been hanging certainly fit that description. Formed from what appeared to be the roots of a cedar tree, it had a classic, broad chandelier shape, illumination provided by fine strands of LED lights that were woven through the root mass, which had been cleaned and coated with a polyurethane that brought out the rich natural color of the wood. He could readily envision a fixture like that for the living room of his cabin.

Hung on the wall nearby, another item sparked his interest—a map of Texas created by cutting the shape of the state out of old, partially rusted and weathered tin roofing, the silhouette mounted on old farm boards.

On the wall behind a rough rawhide sofa, two sections of ladder, hung one above the other, had been fashioned into bookshelves—an airy arrangement that would provide storage without taking up much space in his small cabin. He liked the leather sofa too—comfortable but rugged, a necessary requirement for seating a man who spent much of his day out wrangling cattle.

An old farm table was set up as a dining table, the "chandelier" above it made of a rough-hewn log of mesquite wood wrapped with rope that dangled glass-covered light bulbs. In the corner, what looked like an antique armoire had been made into a buffet, with old baskets storing napkins and rolled place mats, rake heads removed from their handles mounted above them holding wineglasses by their stems, and shelves above that displaying stoneware dishes in neutral colors.

Everywhere he looked, he saw something to intrigue the mind and awaken the senses.

Harrison had nailed his tastes perfectly. Looked like he was going to be spending a lot of money at Hidden Treasures.

In fact, what he really ought to do was hire Abby Rogers to furnish his whole cabin. He loved what she'd collected here, and could envision how great his place would look if she were to take over all of it.

Of course, the fact that it would require Ms. Rogers to come look at his cabin and then consult with him closely during the weeks it took her to find the requisite furnishings made him even surer the idea was brilliant.

Especially if Abby Rogers didn't currently have a man in her life.

Now all he had to do was charm the owner into agreeing.

AS HE WALKED out of the shop, the little girl ran over to him. "Want some of the lemonade I made? Mommy saved you a glass."

"Well, if you made it and she saved it, I'll just have to drink it, won't I?"

He followed the child to the patio, where a full glass awaited him, waving the owner to remain seated when it looked like she was about to get up to greet him.

The child climbed up on the love seat beside her mother and looked at him expectantly. Nothing for it but to take a big sip from the glass.

He was immediately glad he had. "This is delicious—and different! What's in it?"

"Besides lemon, of course, there's mint—we grow it in the garden here."

"It sure is refreshing, especially on a hot afternoon."

"I made good lemonade, didn't I?" the child asked, beaming at him.

"You sure did. But I bet everything you make is good."

Katie nodded solemnly. "Mommy says all my pictures are beautiful too."

Just then, a woman walked out the front door of the house and, seeing the group, paused. "Excuse me for interrupting, but I'd going to head home now, Abby, if that's all right. You'll be out at Marge's tonight? It's pizza night, remember?"

"Aunt Margie said Sissie and I could have ice cream too!" Katie said.

"You sure can. Yes, I'll see you there later, and thanks, Jillee."

"You bet. Bye-bye, Princess," she said to the girl. "I'll see you tonight."

Katie jumped up to give her a hug. "Bye, Miss Jillee."

Nodding to the group, the woman walked over to a car parked under a vine-covered trellis on the far side of the garage, climbed in and drove off.

After finishing her lemonade, Katie carefully put the glass back on the tray. "Can I go finish my drawing, Mommy?"

"Sure, Katie-girl. I'll be inside in a minute, and we'll get ready to go to Aunt Marge's."

"Good! Miss Jillee said Meghan will be there too."

"Two hen parties," Abby said with smile. "The young ones and old ones."

"Nice to meet you, Mr. McAllister," Katie said before skipping off.

"Nice to meet you, too, Princess," he called after her. "She really is a princess," Grant said to her mother after the girl disappeared into the house.

"She is indeed," her mother said with a fond smile. "Though sometimes it seems she's five going on twenty! She's amazing, though. She lights up my world every day."

"Your shop is amazing too."

Looking gratified, she smiled. "Which items did you particularly like?"

"All of them."

She blushed, which Grant found charming. "Thank you."

"Where do you find such unique pieces?"

"I make most of them. Not the leather furniture, though. I order that from a shop in San Antonio. Most of the rest is put together from objects I find in secondhand stores, dumps, yard sales, the side of the road . . . just about anywhere."

"You have a creative and inventive eye, to use things in such unexpected ways. It's sheer genius."

The rosy hue on her cheeks deepened. "I've always liked crafting. When I came to live here, I didn't have much money, so I pretty much had to improvise in order to furnish the house. My husband's family liked what I'd done, bragged on it, had their friends come to see it. Some of them asked me to make similar items for them, and I did. Eventually I decided to open an online shop, and needed a place to photograph and store the objects, so I renovated the garage. Then people started coming out here asking to see them, so the 'storeroom' became a showroom." She laughed. "From a tiny mustard seed . . ."

"Your husband must be proud of you too," he said, knowing he was fishing.

A sadness shadowed her eyes. "I like to think he would be. I . . . lost him several years ago, just before Katie was born."

Grant had the grace to feel guilty. "I'm so sorry. I didn't mean to bring up painful memories."

She took a deep breath, as if gathering herself together,

and gave him a determined smile. "We've made a good life for ourselves, me and Katie. With lots of help from family. I couldn't have done it without the support of my mother-in-law and sister-in-law and their friends. But enough about me. Did you see anything you'd like for your cabin? Most of the items are just display pieces. When someone wants something similar, I make it up on order. Although if you need something immediately, I might be able to let you have the item from the shop."

"Honestly, what I'd really like would be for you to furnish the whole cabin. I've only just started the renovation, so there would be time for you to make as many items as I need. My sister-in-law warned me that most furniture has to be special ordered and recommended I start looking around now, so the pieces would be finished about the same time as the cabin. She's the one who sent me here. Harrison Scott, who just married my brother, Duncan, so she's Harrison McAllister now."

Abby nodded. "I thought I recognized the name. I saw the wedding announcement in the local papers. Her daddy was the one who ran the Scott Ranch, and died suddenly of a heart attack last spring?" When Grant nodded, she added, "I'm sorry for your family's loss."

"It's been hard for her—she and her daddy were very close. I like to think having my brother there has helped her get through it."

"I'm sure it did."

"So—would you be willing to do it? Furnish the whole cabin?"

"Furnish the whole cabin?" she repeated slowly. "How big is it?"

"Not very. Probably about six hundred square feet now, maybe up to one thousand, once I add on two bedrooms and a bathroom."

To Grant's relief, she didn't immediately reject the idea. While he waited with growing anticipation, she appeared to carefully consider it.

"It would be fun to do a whole house again," she said after a moment. "I really enjoyed doing my own. But are you sure you want to turn that much control over the place you'll be living in to someone else?"

"I'd consult closely with you, of course. I like everything I've seen in your shop, but I wouldn't let you put up pink curtains in the kitchen or cover a bedroom dresser with feathers and blingy beads."

"You wouldn't? It takes a real man to carry off pink," she said with a teasing glance.

Grant smiled in delight. That comment and the accompanying glance bordered on the flirtatious. She didn't seem the type to lead a man on, so hopefully that response meant she wasn't involved with anyone. If she agreed to do the cabin, things could only get better.

"I hope I'm man enough to carry off anything."

Laughing, she shook her head at him. "Good. But I

promise to stick with neutral colors."

"That might be better. I'd like things that harmonize with the natural colors and materials that surround the cabin. So—you'll do it?"

"Let me check the order schedule and see how much work I already have lined up. If I think I'll have enough time to fit in furnishing a whole house without falling behind on the projects I've already promised, then yes, I will do it."

"If you need any help with the heavy stuff—I'd really like one of those Texas maps made out of tin roofing—I'd be happy to assist. Cutting the tin for that map couldn't have been easy."

"Thanks, but I can manage. I'm used to being on my own. At first, I didn't have anyone to help, so if I wanted to get something done, I had to figure out how to do it myself. Trial and error, but eventually I found ways to do most everything I needed to do. I have a shop behind the showroom where I do most of the welding, cutting and glasswork. Kept locked, of course, so Katie doesn't wander in and hurt herself."

"A good idea. Cut tin edges can be razor-sharp. When do you think you'll know whether or not you can take on the project?"

"Can I call you tomorrow?"

"You could meet me for dinner."

Her friendly smile disappeared. Her tone noticeably cooler, she said, "Thanks for the offer, but I prefer to keep my personal and professional lives completely separate. If that's a problem, you are still welcome to order pieces from the shop—or take your business elsewhere."

Grant had never thought of himself as irresistible to women. He'd been turned down before—a few times. But he couldn't remember being shut down so quickly and with such finality.

Maybe there was a boyfriend in the wings. Not live-in, he was pretty sure, based on the rather feminine size and character of the furniture on the patio. No rugged, oversized chairs or beer coolers here to indicate a permanent masculine presence.

Alarmed, and hoping to salvage something, he hurried to backtrack. "If I was being overly forward, I'm sorry. I didn't mean to offend you. I just moved back to Whiskey River, and though I grew up here, I've been gone a long time. I don't have many acquaintances here anymore. I admire your skill and I thought maybe we could be . . . friends. But if you'd rather the relationship be strictly professional, I can respect that." *Respect that—but hope to change your mind if I find out you really are available.* "I still want to hire you to furnish my cabin."

She stared at him, as if trying to assess the sincerity of that statement. Grant stared back, hoping she would be convinced.

Not that he could look away anyway. Not only was she achingly lovely, but there was something else, some sort of vulnerability maybe, that called to him. Despite her being a businesswoman, a mother, a widow, there was about her a sense of childlike innocence that activated the same sort of desire to protect that had drawn him to enter the military. It was ridiculous, seeing that he'd only just met her, but beyond the simmering physical desire that made him ache to touch her, he felt the strongest desire to . . . ease her burdens.

So he let himself continue to drink in the beauty of those wide blue eyes, that stubborn, independent chin, that lithe body with tempting curves in all the right places.

"Okay," she said at last with a sharp, quick jerk of her chin. "I'll take you at your word, Grant McAllister. I'll look over the orders tonight and call you tomorrow."

"Don't phone, text me instead. I'll be out cutting hay until late, and cell coverage is spotty in the pastures. I might not be able to receive a phone call, but I'll get the text once I'm in range."

"Very well, I'll text you." She rose and offered her hand. "Thank you for coming by the shop, Mr. McAllister. I hope I can provide what you need for your cabin."

"I'm sure you will." He shook the hand she extended, feeling again that spark of connection—and noting that she broke the contact much more quickly than she had the first time.

*She feels it too—even if she won't acknowledge it.*

"Until tomorrow, then," she said. "Safe drive home."

"Thank you. I'll look forward to hearing from you."

Giving him another nod, she turned and walked back to the house.

With no excuse to remain, he headed to his truck, watching out of the corner of his eye until Abby Rogers disappeared inside. What he wanted from that intriguing blonde went far beyond a chandelier and a leather sofa.

He would have liked to linger with her on the patio, maybe follow up the lemonade with a beer or a glass of wine. Get to know more about her and her unique skill. How she came to Whiskey River, and why she'd stayed.

She couldn't be more than thirty, if that. She must have been in her early twenties when she was widowed. And how had that happened?

He sure hoped she decided to take on the project. Despite their disappointing start, he still wanted to see way more of Abby Rogers. And until he had solid confirmation that she was involved with someone, he wouldn't give up—yet—on persuading her to do more than just furnish his cabin.

# Chapter Three

LATER THAT EVENING on the other side of Whiskey River, Abby Rogers sat out on her sister-in-law, Marge's, deck, wineglass in hand, enjoying the beauty of the sunset over the hills of the Balcones Escarpment. After sending Jillee, the third member of their babysitting co-op, off to do the errands she wanted to run while they supervised the children, she and Marge had migrated outdoors to enjoy the peace and quiet. Inside, Katie and her six-year-old cousin, Sissie, were playing "school" with Jillee's daughter, Meghan, at age twelve the "older woman" the two younger girls looked up to with awe.

"You're looking a little peaked this evening," Abby said to Marge, who'd just returned to the deck with a fresh bottle of wine. "Out late last night?"

"Yes, some friends from the office went out for drinks after work."

A little concerned, Abby put a hand on Marge's arm. "Are you sure it isn't too much, you coming over to help me with the bookkeeping after pulling a full day at Kelly Boots?"

"No, it's fine," Marge assured her. "I only come by two

evenings a week, and after being in daycare all day, you know Sissie loves to play with Katie."

"Those two do make a team," Abby said, nodding toward the chatter coming from inside the house. "Cousins who are close as sisters. I'm so grateful Katie has Sissie."

"They do get along brilliantly," Marge said. "Even better when Meghan joins them. They love following her around."

"So where did you go? Booze's?"

"No, Buddy's. Have you been there yet?"

When Abby shook her head, Marge continued, "It's that new place on RR2766, in a former gas station. Great draft beer, Hill Country wine, and country music—Buddy gets in some terrific bands. You should come honkytonking with us some night."

"Who would watch the kids?"

"You know Mom would. Think about it," Marge coaxed.

Abby nodded, but she knew she wouldn't. Five years as a widow had hardly eased the searing sense of loss. With a swooping feeling in her stomach, she recalled the awful day when she'd answered a knock at the door of her small apartment in base housing to find on her doorstep a Marine in full dress uniform, trailed by the chaplain. She'd known even before she invited them in that they'd come to tell her Ross wouldn't be coming home again.

She'd been newly pregnant. Sick, scared, and alone. Abandoned.

It had taken her years to battle back and reclaim her independence and a fragile sense of stability. She never intended to risk that again.

"You will really think about it, won't you?" Marge persisted.

"Probably not," she admitted. "Besides, I might cramp your style if you're trying to hook up with some hot new man."

"Hot new man?" Marge laughed. "Pretty slim pickings in Whiskey River. Most of the hot men here are either married or already taken. The girls and I just like to go dance, have a few beers and relax."

"I already have Jillee watching Katie a couple times a week while I'm in the workshop. I don't like to leave her too often."

"Same old excuse," Marge said, shaking her head. "You're hopeless. Anyway, although he wasn't present, some of the girls *were* all aflutter about the hot new man who just moved back to town."

When Abby returned a noncommittal murmur, Marge sighed. "Your lack of interest in hot men borders on the sinful, you know. You've been widowed long enough to not feel guilty about expressing *interest*. You don't have to do anything about it. Besides, you know my brother wouldn't have wanted you to live like a nun for the rest of your life."

No, Ross would have wanted her to embrace life with exuberance—like he had. Live every day to the fullest. And she tried to, sharing joy every day with Katie. She just didn't want her happiness to depend on a man again. Someone who might send her world into a tailspin if he suddenly left it.

When Abby remained silent, Marge said, "Very well. Since you won't ask, I'll tell you anyway. It's Grant McAllister. His brother Duncan runs the Triple A Ranch. He, Grant, and their younger brother, Brice, are about the three hunkiest siblings in the history of mankind. Oh, my, the hearts that fluttered every time they walked down the hall in high school! Though the women of the world have lost one—Duncan got married earlier this month."

Abby debated returning just another monosyllabic response. But saying nothing might come back to bite her in the butt if her sister-in-law later discovered she'd already met Grant McAllister and neglected to mention it.

Because he really was hot. The immediate physical response she'd felt had been as strong as it was unexpected and unwelcome. Her sister-in-law was certain to speculate about that response unless she dealt with it immediately.

So, after taking another sip from her wineglass, she said, "As it turns out, I've already met the Hot New Man. He stopped by the shop today. And you're right," she added reluctantly. "He is very kind on the eye."

"Be still, my heart! So you aren't dead yet," Marge said. "What brought him to the shop?"

"He said he's renovating a cabin and was looking for things to furnish it."

"Looks like Jane Wilson was right, then! She told Maggie at Tips, Tops & Toes when she was getting her nails done that Grant is moving back to Whiskey River permanently. She said that since Duncan and Harrison's marriage have reunited the two sections of the old Triple A ranch, Duncan needed someone to help him run it—and he'd asked Grant to come home and manage the Scott half."

"He was gone for a while, I take it," Abby said. Though she hadn't much interest in town gossip, and even less in available men, Marge seemed enthused, making her feel obligated to keep the conversation going.

"Yes. He left right after we all graduated from high school, much to sorrow of Desiré Ames, his high school flame."

"'Desiré?' Seriously?"

"Well, her given name is 'Sally,' but she after she got over Grant leaving, she went on to model in Dallas. Needed a more glamorous name, she said. Nobody wanted to hire a model named 'Sally' to do sexy lingerie ads."

"So cowboy-hero-handsome Grant left town for greener pastures too. Not wanting to be encumbered by his old girlfriend. Did he go into modeling or Hollywood?"

Marge laughed. "Grant? Oh, no! He might be handsome enough, and he *was* a cowboy—one of the top high school saddle bronc riders in the state. But he didn't have any interest in joining the circuit professionally. He always talked about going places and seeing the world once he got out of high school, and he knew Duncan would take care of the ranch. Like Ross, he joined the Marines. Spent eight years in the Corps, though they weren't in the same branch. Grant was Recon."

A familiar dull ache of loss and pain resonated through Abby. Pressing her lips together to keep from uttering the negative retort that first sprang to mind, she once again resorted to a noncommittal murmur.

A former Marine. Yet another reason to resist the appeal of Grant McAllister.

"I always wondered if they met up somewhere while they were both in the Corps," Marge was saying.

"I didn't recognize the name, so probably not. The Marines are a pretty big outfit."

"True, but they tend to be close, don't they? Once a Marine, always a Marine, *Oo-rah,* and all that?"

"Yes, most of them feel a special bond with fellow Marines."

*A special bond that excluded all but the warriors.*

"Well, I for one am happy to have him back in Whiskey River. You should be too. And he's going to buy some things from the shop? That means you'll see more of him, right?"

"Probably. He did seem very interested in several items."

She didn't want to mention—yet—his request that she oversee the furnishing of his whole cabin. Even though before coming here tonight, she'd had a look at her order book and decided she'd have enough time to take on the project. She knew she would enjoy the challenge and opportunity to redo an entire dwelling. The only thing making her hesitate was that alarming surge of response to Grant McAllister.

Who, if his siblings were equally handsome, truly must be one of the three hunkiest brothers in the history of mankind.

"Did he seem . . . interested? Much as you downplay your looks, you really are beautiful. And you definitely need to get out more. Unless he's changed radically since high school, Grant is not only easy on the eye, he's a nice guy too."

Abby sighed with exasperation. This was old ground they'd gone over too many times. "Marge, you know I'm not interested in dating. The guy you set me up with last year was nice, but I'd just as soon spend any free time I have with you, the girls or Katie."

"Okay, so he wasn't nice enough to tempt you to see him again. It wouldn't hurt to try someone else, you know. Katie's older now, she doesn't need you 24/7, like she did when she was a baby. I'd be happy to watch her if you wanted to go out some night. You need to, before you forget how to be a woman."

Abby laughed. "I don't think it's something a girl forgets."

"You know what I mean. Forget how to dress up in something tight and sexy, how to put on makeup that makes your blue eyes look even more enormous. Forget how to flirt with a guy. How to enjoy a little humpty-bumpty in the night."

"I think I've done well enough without a man for five years," she retorted. Despite being lonely. In spite of desperately missing the closeness and passion of intimacy. But she'd survived, defiant in the face of her mother's prediction that she'd not last six months on her own.

"Why don't you drop Sissie over with us? *You* can go out and find someone and enjoy some humpty-bumpty in the night," she countered.

"I wouldn't mind spending an evening gazing into Grant McAllister's soulful blue eyes, but nothing more for me—not yet. I'm still not over finding that cheating bum of an ex-husband doing the dirty with that trashy blonde from Last Stand—in my very own bed! If I could have gotten to my purse fast enough, I would have shot the bastard. I'm just glad the divorce went through quickly and he left Whiskey River. I only have to see him when I drop off Sissie for her weekends."

It was a perfect opening to finally reveal to Marge her own awful experience, the biggest reason she wasn't ready to date—that dreadful, grief-induced hookup she'd had soon after learning of Ross's death. Marge probably wouldn't criticize her for hopping into bed with a near-stranger within a week of learning she'd been widowed, but she'd always been too embarrassed and ashamed to admit that lapse to the doting sister who'd loved Ross as much as she had.

The very idea of dating still brought back memories of the agonized regret she'd felt when she woke the next morning—and the even worse feeling that she'd betrayed Ross and their love. Maybe someday those memories would finally fade—but they hadn't yet.

She opened her lips, then closed them. Though confessing would help her sister-in-law to better understand her reluctance, she still couldn't bring herself to do it.

"Why don't we both stay as we are?" she suggested instead. "Men just . . . complicate things. I'm a firm believer in girlfriend power!"

"Girlfriend power and sisterhood!" Marge agreed, clinking her wineglass with Abby's. "But complicating as they are, men sure can be fun to cozy up with."

In spite of herself, distant memories of lying entangled with Ross in their bed, memories of intoxicating pleasure and the sweet aftermath of lovemaking, crept into her mind. A wave of bittersweet longing washed through her as she thought again of all she had lost. The best friend she'd ever had. Her one true love.

No, even after the bad memories faded, she doubted she would ever encounter a man who could replace Ross.

"For now, I don't need any more complications. You know I spend most evenings after Katie goes to bed working to complete orders. I don't have time to date, even if I had the inclination. Maybe someday, once the business is more established . . ."

Finally, thankfully, Marge let the subject drop. Nodding, she said, "Okay. Sisterhood for now. Should we go in and set the girls up with a movie? With school tomorrow, Jillee will want to take Meghan home as soon as she gets back so she doesn't get to bed too late, and you know the girl won't want to leave before the movie ends."

"Yes, let's go set it up. I think our choices are going to be from among two or three Disney princesses."

"Probably," Marge said with a laugh. "I have to bribe Sissie out of her costume when she wants to play outdoors. Speaking of 'costumes,' have you gotten any more packages from your mother this week?"

Abby groaned. "Thankfully, no. It's like after 'suddenly' rediscovering she has a grandchild, she's trying to make up for lost time, sending all those expensive toys and fancy dresses Katie doesn't need. Or maybe she's just trying to not-so-subtly remind me that she can afford to buy things that are way out of my price range. It would be par for the course for her to try to rub my nose in how my choice of husband left me far less well-off than my parents, just as she predicted."

"You're welcome to bring anything you don't want over here," Marge said with a grin. "I'll be happy to take advantage of your mother's ugly-motivated generosity."

"I'll keep that in mind," Abby said acerbically as she hefted the wine bottle and grabbed her glass. "After you."

"Once we get the movie running, I'll cut up some more cheese to go with this wine, if you'd like more."

"Willingly," Abby said as she held open the door for her friend.

Smiling at the girlish chatter she heard coming from Sissie's bedroom, while Marge proceeded into the kitchen, Abby went over to pull several movie selections out of the cabinet in the family room. How the girls did love their princesses!

Who didn't love being rescued by a handsome prince?

But she'd left fairy-tale endings behind long ago, when she lost her own prince. Still, despite pain and loss, she was profoundly grateful for the blessings life had brought her way.

Her wonderful, magical little daughter who brightened her world every day. A business that was finally beginning to bring in enough income that she no longer had to depend wholly on her small widow's pension. Good friends like Marge, Jillee, and her mother-in-law, Helen. A snug home and a creatively satisfying job.

Before she allowed another man in her life, she wanted to build that business into a resounding success, to prove to herself as much as to her mother that she was strong enough to not only survive on her own, but to thrive.

Until then, she didn't need dancing at honky-tonks, gazing into the eyes of hot men, or stepping out with Grant McAllister.

JUST AFTER DAWN the following morning, Abby took her fresh cup of coffee out to the terrace. She loved this time of day, the peace and stillness before Katie woke up and the nonstop activity of a day supervising an energetic five-year-old began.

She never tired of watching the sun rise pink and golden from behind the eastern hills, its beauty renewed each morning.

Though she'd grown up in Dallas, not all that far from the Hill Country, until she came here, grieving and broken, to her husband's hometown, she'd never visited this part of Texas, despite the fact that both her parents were wine enthusiasts. Though the region had received considerable acclaim for the vintages produced by its many vineyards, her fashionable mother wouldn't have deigned to drink something locally produced. Nothing less than a Bordeaux from a famous French label would do for Gwenneth Richardson.

Abby had fallen instantly in love with the rugged terrain, the golden stone and scrub mesquite, the valleys dotted with streams and wildflowers, the tall hills crested by old-growth cypress and live oak. It was a land of wide vistas, an open land one could breathe in. A land in which one could recreate a life.

As she had.

Soon, Jillee would arrive to watch Katie while Abby

worked in the shop. She'd better go back in and make a new pot so she'd have a cup ready for Jillee, extra blond with two sweeteners, just like her own. And while the coffee brewed, she'd text Grant McAllister to accept his offer that she oversee the furnishing of his cabin.

After returning from Marge's last night, she'd lain awake for a long time, mulling over whether or not she should take the job. She'd finally decided that it would be silly to turn down a lucrative commission—and the chance to take Instagram photos of its progress to post on her social media and business pages, which would certainly generate interest from prospective customers.

Completing an entire house would allow her to expand her portfolio and perhaps lead to other whole-house projects, a faster way toward her goal of a successful business than working on single pieces. It wouldn't make good financial sense to refuse just because, for the first time since Ross's death, she'd encountered a man who tempted her to emerge from her self-imposed celibacy.

She still had her work and Katie to occupy her. Surely she was mature enough, and professional enough, not to allow the desire Grant McAllister aroused in her to get in the way of completing the project. Or complicate her life.

# Chapter Four

A S THE HOT summer sun burned low in the western sky three days later, Abby loaded Katie up in her old pickup and headed out to the McAllister ranch. After an exchange of texts, she'd agreed to meet Grant McAllister at the cabin he was renovating on the eastern edge of the ranch property. He'd texted her a map with a pin, telling her the cabin wasn't that difficult to find, but commercial GPS systems didn't always give the correct directions.

"We're going to see a cabin, Mommy?" Katie asked.

"Yes, Katie-girl. Mr. McAllister's cabin. You remember him—he came by the shop a few days ago."

Katie nodded as Abby checked to make sure her daughter had her safety harness correctly in place. "He had a nice smile. And pretty blue eyes. And he liked my lemonade."

"Who wouldn't like your lemonade? It's delicious!"

"Is the cabin made out of logs? Miss Jillee read me a story about the first people who came to Texas. She said they lived in cabins."

"Mr. Grant told me his grandfather built the cabin, but I don't know if it's made of logs or not," Abby said as she popped her phone into the holder, activated the GPS map she'd been sent, and climbed up to fasten her own seat belt.

"Miss Jillee said the cabin is up on a hill and there's a river at the bottom. Can I swim after we look at the cabin?"

"Not swim, but if it's okay with Mr. Grant, we can put on our water shoes and wade in the shallows. I packed us some drinks and a snack. We could have a little picnic."

"Yeah! I love picnics!" Katie cried, clapping her hands.

"How about we have a picnic, no matter what?" Abby said, smiling at the image of her daughter in the rearview mirror and always happy to offer her little girl a treat— especially one that didn't put a strain on the family budget. "If we can't go to the river there, we'll stop by the park in Whiskey River on the way home. Would you like that?"

"I'd love that, Mommy! Why do we need to see Mr. Grant's cabin?"

"Nobody has lived in it for a long time. He's fixing it up and then he'll need furniture and lights and things."

Katie nodded. "You make the best lights and things. I love my teacup lamp. It's pink and pretty."

Abby smiled, remembering Grant's comment about pink. "Mr. Grant will probably want something more . . . manly."

Now that she'd gotten past her indecision about whether or not it was wise to do the project, she was looking forward to it with enthusiasm. Walking through the cabin, seeing the materials it was made of, getting an idea of the intended floor plan, knowing what its surroundings looked like, would all guide her to recommend pieces tailored just to that dwelling, and probably inspire her to create new works designed specifically for that space and setting.

While Katie chattered away in the back seat, Abby watched the road and the GPS. About half an hour after leaving Whiskey River, she turned into the long drive leading to the Scott ranch house, then branched off before reaching the house itself on another dirt road leading due east. Fifteen minutes of slow driving after that, just as Grant's instructions had predicted, she saw on a ridge in the distance a small cabin silhouetted against the sky.

A few minutes later, they reached the spot. After parking her truck next to Grant's on a graveled area beside the cabin, she hopped out while Katie scrambled down from her car seat. Grant McAllister didn't come to meet them, but the roar of a chainsaw from the other side of the cabin confirmed he was somewhere on the site.

As they rounded the corner, Abby stopped short. Grant was there, all right—using the chainsaw to cut up a large cedar tree, which filled the air with its fragrance. Despite the late-afternoon heat, he wore a helmet with a protective face shield, chainsaw chaps, and heavy gloves. But in deference to the temperature, he'd rolled up the sleeves of his chambray work shirt, displaying impressive biceps, while sweat plastered the shirt itself to his back and his broad shoulders.

Having apparently not heard them approach, he shut

down the chainsaw and set it down, then stripped off his helmet and shirt—displaying a strong masculine back as impressive as his biceps.

Abby felt her stomach swoop as that long-buried physical response stirred again. After skipping a beat, her heart tripped back into rhythm.

Okay, she told herself as she blew out a shaky breath, it had been a long time since she'd felt such an immediate physical response. But that was no excuse to hyperventilate like a concert groupie sighting her favorite rock star.

Fortunately oblivious to the effect Grant McAllister was having on her mother, Katie ran toward him. "We're here, Mr. Grant! What are you making?"

STARTLED, GRANT TURNED quickly and spotted them. He also caught her frankly staring at him. With a pleased little smile, he picked up his shirt and put it back on—but slowly, so she had plenty of time to appreciate the view.

"Hello, Princess," he said, looking away from Abby to smile at Katie. "I'm going to make a bench for my front porch out of this cedar log."

Irritated with herself that he'd been able to read her reaction, Abby felt her face heat. Ross had always teased that she was a terrible poker player, her emotions clearly visible on her face. She scrambled to think of something to shut down that avenue of conversation if he made any comment about her evident appreciation. If she were to do this job, she needed to insist the tone of their interactions be professional from the very beginning.

But to her relief—since she'd not yet thought of any suitable remarks—McAllister kept his attention on Katie.

"The wood smells good," Katie said. "My mommy is good at making things too."

"Cedar does smell good, doesn't it? And your mommy sure does make nice things. That's why I wanted her to come and see my cabin. So she can make some nice things for it."

By this time, Abby had reached the porch. "Hello, Mr. McAllister," she said, pleased, despite her still-unsteady pulse, to produce a cool, professional tone. She was also smart enough this time not to offer him her hand to shake.

"I'd rather it be 'Grant,' if that's okay. We're not so formal here in the country, even doing business."

"Okay . . . Grant."

"By the way, thanks for driving all the way out," he replied, his friendly smile devoid of any flirtatious overtones.

Feeling a little easier, Abby said, "You're welcome. But it was no trouble. I need to see a project in its setting to have a better feel for what will work."

"Are we going to see your cabin now?" Katie asked.

"As soon as your mommy is ready," he replied.

For, having pulled her gaze away from the attractive man before her, she'd finally taken in the setting, and was gazing around, awestruck.

The cabin was indeed perched on a ridge—and the view was spectacular. The vista overlooked the surrounding countryside, with the steeper hills of the Balcones Escarpment to the north and the smaller ones stretching east toward New Braunfels. Below the porch on the front of the cabin was a small, flat terrace bordered by large, irregular rocks, after which the land fell away sharply. Far below, to the north, then east, then south, a thin ribbon of river snaked along the canyon bottom.

"Wow!" she breathed. "I understand now why you wanted to live out here!"

"It's beautiful, isn't it? Granddaddy knew what he was doing when he rebuilt the log cabin *his* grandfather erected when he first settled here. It was a defensible spot then, which was important, because there were still periodic raids by the Comanche. Later, when the land was secured, Granddaddy built a new house that my brother and his wife live in now, on the western side of the ranch where it's not as rocky and the pasturage is better. But he kept this place as a hunting cabin. No one has used it for over ten years, so it's in need of work, but the basic structure is sound."

Katie, unimpressed by vistas, was fidgeting on the deck. "Can we go inside now, Mommy?"

"Go ahead, Princess," Grant told her, and then turned to Abby as Katie scampered inside. "Ready? Don't want to keep your chaperone waiting."

Just when she'd decided he wasn't going to say something to fluster her, he caught her off guard. Especially since he was more than half right.

Jillee had offered to stay later and watch Katie while she drove out, but Abby had wanted to bring her. Because her daughter liked going places and seeing new things, but also to make sure she had some reinforcement in resisting Grant McAllister. Just in case he decided to act on the response she'd just demonstrated he could produce in her.

Before she could master her renewed annoyance and come up with an appropriate comeback, he held up a hand. "No more teasing. I'm glad you brought Katie. She's a delight. Besides, children are so honest. I'll be real interested in what she thinks of the cabin. And what you think, of course."

Walking ahead, he pushed back the door and waved her in.

She went in, discovering the interior to be one large, open room; its walls made of pale, native limestone rocks, its cedar beamed ceiling open to the roof.

"I've just removed the old ceiling so I could vault the room, which lightened things up a lot," Grant said, pointing upward. "I'm going to keep the heart-of-pine floors, but I'm still waiting on the stone mason to come out and help me enlarge the window openings on either side of the front door, so you can see out to the porch and the vista beyond. I'll be putting in a kitchen against that back, western wall," he continued, pointing, "with a dining table there, by the south wall. I'll be adding two windows on either side of the fireplace on the north wall too. The front deck will continue and wrap around the north side, and beyond that back door on the western wall, I'm going to build an addition with two bedrooms and a bathroom. There'll be another deck off the north bedroom to take advantage of the view where the river curves around to the north."

"It's already beautiful," Abby said. "Opening up the ceiling makes it feel so airy, and once you have more windows, the interior will be flooded with light."

Grant nodded. "Just the way I like it."

Having wandered around the room, out the back door and back inside, Katie said, "You don't have any furniture."

"Not yet. Your mommy's going to help me pick some out. But first, I have to build the kitchen and then, out that door you just came back in, a bathroom and bedrooms."

"I like it," Katie announced. "The stone is pretty. It's like a castle on top of this big hill."

"What will you do for water, electricity, and sewage?" Abby asked.

"Great-granddaddy had a well dug, so there's good water; I just need a modern, more efficient pump. I'll be installing a septic system to the west beyond the new bathroom and solar panels on the roof for electricity, with a gas generator for backup."

"Sounds well-thought-out," Abby said as she paced the

space, making mental notes of its size, the coloring of the stone of the walls and fireplace, the pine floor, the cedar roof beams.

"What are you envisioning for the kitchen?"

"A wall of cabinets going up to ceiling height, with the gas stove on the western wall, an island with a sink overlooking the rest of the room."

"What style and color of cabinets?"

"Not too modern, not too rustic. Maybe a plain Craftsman style, the wood whitewashed to let the grain show through. Patterned-tile backsplash, something in muted tans and grays, maybe with a little blue. Quartz countertops for the kitchen and bathroom, maybe in a concrete gray."

She nodded. "Leather sofa and chairs for seating by the fireplace?"

"Yes. Comfortable and durable. I don't want to have to baby furniture or worry about spilling a beer on it. I really liked the cypress–root chandelier you had in the shop. I can envision that in front of the fireplace. That log-and-bottle light over the dining table, and maybe some industrial-style lights over the kitchen island. Ladder bookcases on the far wall. A buffet like the one in the shop to hold linens and bar items."

"What do you envision for the bedrooms?"

"They'll be framed out in wood, probably shiplap walls painted white. Just room enough for bed, dresser, and bedside tables. The living and relaxing will be done in the main room or on the decks."

"Antique iron beds?"

He nodded. "Yes, I'd like that."

"When do you think you'll have the cabin ready for lighting fixtures and furniture?"

"I'll be doing most of the work myself, so probably two-to-three months at the earliest."

"Good. That will give me plenty of time to get the chairs and sofas on order and to explore my various sources to turn up bedframes, tables, dressers and buffets. Once you have the addition roughed in and the windows finished in here, I can take another look to get a feel for dimensions. Do you want me to source rugs, curtains, and linens as well?"

"Yes, and a lot more. I've rented out my condo in San Antonio furnished, so I'll be needing everything from towels to bedspreads to kitchen knives."

"And your budget?"

He named a figure that had Abby nodding. "Good. I should be able to work with that. I'll make up some preliminary design sketches to show you before I order—or start making—anything and have them ready in, say, a week?"

"That would be great. I know you'll make the place look unbelievable."

"With this site and this beautiful stone to work with, it shouldn't be too difficult. Pretty much anything you put in here will be beautified."

"Mommy, are we ready to go to the river now?" Katie

asked.

"Yes, Katie-girl, we're almost finished." Looking over to Grant, she said, "Marge told me about the river at the boundary of the ranch. If you don't mind, I wanted to take Katie down and let her go wading."

"Sure. After that chainsawing, I wouldn't mind wading a little myself."

A sudden vision of Grant McAllister stripped down and standing in the river, water rippling off his muscles and strong, tanned legs, dried her mouth and robbed her temporarily of speech.

Having him accompany them was *so* not a good idea.

Unfortunately, before she could say anything, Katie piped up, "Will you go wading with us? Mommy brought drinks and snacks too!"

"Thanks for the invitation, Princess, but your mommy wasn't planning on feeding an extra person." As if sensing she wasn't truly comfortable including him in the excursion, he continued, "I'll just show you the way down. You can't drive there, but there's a path that runs diagonally down the slope, so it's not too steep."

"Come on, Mommy, let's go!" Katie said, running over to grab her hand. "I can't wait to see the river."

Abby didn't see a way to refuse his escort now—or make an excuse to get out of going at all—without hugely disappointing her daughter. "Are you sure it won't be too much trouble?" she asked, grasping at the last straw.

"Not a bit. That section of river is one of my favorite places on the ranch. Just let me grab some water from the well and rinse off, and I'll take you down. You can wait out on the porch if you like."

"Thanks, we will."

"We need to get our drinks and our snacks," Katie reminded. "I'm hungry and thirsty!"

Resigned to the inevitable, while Katie skipped ahead of her, Abby walked back to her truck and pulled out the cooler with drinks, yogurt, cheese, fruit, a picnic basket containing plates, cutlery and napkins, and her backpack with towels and shoes. By the time she got back to the porch, Grant McAllister had come back out, attired in a clean tee shirt—which once again displayed those impressive biceps—a pair of battered shorts and hiking boots.

He'd thrown some water on his face and slicked back his wavy, dark hair. With those—what had Marge called them, "soulful?"—blue eyes, winning smile and impressive physique, he looked like the picture beside the dictionary definition of "temptation to end chastity."

Not that she intended to succumb to it. That road led to far more complications than she cared to contemplate, especially with the project looming. Which she really was enthusiastic about undertaking. She didn't want to make the numerous consultations she would need to have with the owner awkward or unpleasant because she'd taken a step she couldn't take back.

While they walked down the trail, which was as gentle as McAllister had promised, Katie fired a stream of questions at him about the river. Did it have fish? ("It does.") Were there good rocks to skip, like Jillee's daughter, Meghan, had showed her? ("There are.") Was it was deep enough to swim in or only deep enough for wading? ("Wading only at this point.") After a few minutes' walk, they arrived at a small, flat, grassy spot beside a rock-bordered, lazily moving stream.

Pointing toward a large, flat rock near the water's edge, Grant said, "That would be a good spot to lay out your picnic gear. You can wade into the stream anywhere along here. The riverbed is mostly sandy, though there are rocks that can be sharp. Did you bring water shoes?"

"Yes," she said with a nod. "I'll get them out."

"I'll put mine on, Mommy," Katie said as Abby unzipped the backpack. "Are you wading too, Mr. Grant? Please say yes! You can skip stones with me. I bet you skip stones better than Meghan."

Before replying, he looked over to Abby, a question in his eyes.

Appreciating that he was allowing her to make the decision rather than letting Katie force her hand, she said, "We don't want to keep you from whatever else you might need to do. But if you have the time, please stay."

# Chapter Five

ABBY HAD TO smile to herself as the words left her lips. She would never have predicted while she was driving over this afternoon that she'd actually be inviting Grant McAllister to spend time with them.

"I'd enjoy staying, if you're sure that's okay. I wouldn't want to barge in on you sharing a special time with your daughter."

As he gazed at her, she felt again the connection pulling at her—physical, yes, but more than just that. She found, somewhat to her dismay, that she *liked* being around him.

Which ought to be reason enough for her to rescind the permission she'd just given—but that would disappoint Katie, who was waiting expectantly for her rock-slinging companion to escort her into the river.

Gesturing to her daughter, she said, "I think Katie's more excited to skip rocks with you than she is to wade with me."

He smiled. "Are you coming in too?"

"Of course. I didn't do much river-wading as a child. Katie loves it, and I'm making up for lost time."

He waited while she tied the laces on her shoes and checked Katie's, then led them into the water. "Aren't you going to ruin your boots?" she asked.

"No, these are designed so they can get wet. Much easier in the summer to wear lighter-weight boots rather than leather, and you never know when you might have to haul some cow out of a boggy spot. Where did you grow up that didn't allow you to go wading?" he asked as he escorted them along the shallows.

"Dallas."

"Ah. City girl?"

"I was until I married. Then we moved around from base to base, some of which were in the country. Then, after my husband's death, we moved here. I love the area," she said simply.

"As a Hill Country boy, born and bred, I'm not going to argue with you there. From base to base, you said? My brother Duncan reminded me that I went to school with Marge, but Ross was several years younger, so I didn't know him well. I seem to remember my brother, Brice, who played lineman, saying he was a good football player, but I didn't know he'd joined up."

She took a deep breath. Might as well get the painful part over quickly. "He was a Marine. Like you. Thank you for your service, by the way."

He nodded, studying her face. "He died on active duty?"

"Afghanistan. His third tour, which was going to be his

last. Well, it was his last, all right." *His last anything. Their last everything.* She took a ragged breath against the pain that five years had only muted.

"I'm so sorry," he said quietly.

Nodding, she looked away from the sympathy in his eyes. "These look like good stones for skipping, Katie." Picking up several, she handed them to her daughter. "Remember, you move your arm sideways, like Meghan showed you, not over your head."

Tacitly accepting that she didn't want to discuss the matter further, Grant leaned down to get his own supply of rocks. After Katie threw several—all of them hitting the water and immediately sinking, Grant walked over to the girl. "Can I help you throw?"

After she nodded, Grant knelt down and positioned Katie in front of him. "Choose your smoothest, flattest rock."

"This one?" she asked.

"That looks good. Now, I'm going to help you move your arm back, like this," he said, suiting action to words. "Then, on the count of three, we're going to sling your arm forward so you can throw the stone. Ready?"

After she nodded enthusiastically, Grant drew her little arm back. "Okay. One, two, three—throw!"

With his help, Katie managed to throw the stone five or six feet away—and skim it twice across the river surface before it sank.

Turning around, a look of delight on her face, she cried, "Mommy, did you see? I did it! It skipped two whole times!"

"Great job, Katie-girl," Abby said, smiling at her daughter's enthusiasm.

"Can we do it again, Mr. Grant?" Katie asked.

"As many times as you want."

"You may regret that answer," Abby said with a laugh. "Katie can be very focused when she wants to do something."

He merely nodded. "Takes practice to become an expert stone-slinger. Ready, Katie?"

HALF AN HOUR later, while with wonderful patience, Grant continued to skip stones with Katie, Abby changed back into her tennis shoes and went over to set out the picnic on the flat rock he'd indicated. After spreading out the blanket and pulling out snacks, cups, and water, she called, "Ready to eat, Katie?"

"Mr. Grant, are you going to eat with us too?"

"I don't want to eat up your provisions," he said, looking over at Abby. "I'm sure you weren't planning on having a guest."

Once again, he was letting her set the boundaries—not trying to use the attraction he must know she felt to coax her.

Which made her feel a bit easier, as well as grateful. And heck—she wanted him to stay too.

"I always have extra water, there's plenty of cheese, and I brought the whole box of crackers. You're welcome to some, if you like. After all, a champion rock-slinger deserves a treat."

He smiled. "If you don't mind, I'd be happy to stay."

"Can I skip ten more stones first?" Katie asked.

"How about five? I bet Mr. Grant is thirsty and is wanting some water."

The requisite rocks tossed, Katie hopped out of the water and came over to the blanket, changing into her dry shoes at her mother's reminder, then sitting down to open the yogurt container and the water Abby handed her.

Settling his wet boots off the blanket, Grant took a seat beside her daughter.

"The beautiful setting probably deserves wine, but this will have to do," she said, offering him a bottle of water. "Help yourself to the cheese and crackers."

"Thanks." Popping the top on the water, he drank down nearly half.

He even looked sexy while drinking water, Abby thought with a sigh. She was going to have to be extra vigilant during this project to keep herself from getting into trouble.

*Job number one—building the business*, she reminded herself.

"Wine would be better, but this water is good," he said,

reaching over to take a few crackers and some cheese.

"This sure is a beautiful spot. You grew up here, didn't you?"

"Yes, we roamed the area pretty freely all through school. Used to stay in the cabin often during hunting season—there's lots of deer on the eastern hills. Sometimes my brothers and I spent the weekend chasing squirrels or jackrabbits. Daddy didn't like us hunting closer to the pastures—gunfire upsets the cattle."

"Your dad too busy with ranch chores to hunt with you?"

"He came out, too, during deer season. But he died as we were just entering high school. Our stepmom tried to keep the ranch going, but after a couple of bad years, she was forced to sell off the eastern half of the original Triple A. The new owner—my sister-in-law's daddy—never used the cabin, which is why it was in such rough shape. After they married, Harrison and Duncan merged the two properties, giving us access to the eastern half of the ranch again—and the cabin. When Duncan asked me to move back and help him with the ranch, I knew this was where I wanted to live."

"You're not living in it now, surely!"

"Actually, I'd planned to, but Harrison asked me to stay at her daddy's place while I was doing the renovations. Didn't want his house to sit unoccupied, which I can understand. And, much as I love camping, I have to admit that it's nice after a long day cutting hay and chasing cows to come back to a hot shower, eat a dinner I don't have to build a fire to cook, maybe watch a movie, and sleep in an air-conditioned bedroom."

"My preferred version of camping."

He chuckled. "It's also convenient being there, since Harrison wanted me to keep the horses exercised. I may build a small stable behind the cabin eventually and bring a couple of them over here, once I move in. It will be nice to have horses around again. We had to sell off all of ours when we sold the land—even my rodeo mount. It was hard letting Shadow go, but horses are expensive—shoeing, vet bills, feed. I already knew I'd be leaving the area after high school anyway, and all the money we could scrape together had to go to support the rest of the ranch."

"Marge told me that you rode broncs in high school. On a borrowed horse?"

"Our high school coach bought Shadow and let me use him until I moved away."

"That was considerate of him."

Grant laughed. "It was—but he was also determined to keep me in rodeo, since I'd placed so high in the junior competitions. I thanked him by winning the state championship my last two years in high school."

"As a saddle bronc rider? I'm in awe! I have enough trouble staying on the back of one that's *not* bucking."

His eyes lit. "You ride, then?"

"I've done a little riding. I wouldn't say I'm competent."

"You'll have to come riding with me and let me show you around the ranch someday. The best way to see the land is from horseback. It'll give you a better feel for this area, maybe some more inspiration about furnishings."

Abby laughed. "Only if you have a slug who hardly breaks a walk!"

Grant smiled. "I can probably arrange that."

"Maybe I will, then."

Abby hadn't thought that Katie, busy eating her snack, was paying much attention to the adult conversation, but at that, she said, "Mommy, can I ride horses too?"

"I'd be happy to show you how to ride, Princess, but I don't have a pony now. The horses on the ranch would be too big for you."

"Can you teach me to ride when I'm bigger?"

Before Abby could stop her daughter from asking for favors, Katie's attention was diverted by a school of small fish darting around the edge of their picnic rock. "Look, Mommy! Fishies!"

"Those are little ones, but farther down the river, where it gets deeper, there are bigger fish," Grant said. "When we stayed at the cabin, my brothers and I used to catch some and fry them up for dinner."

"I'd like to catch a fish! Can you take me?"

"Katie!" Abby said in a warning tone. "Mr. Grant is busy taking care of his ranch. He doesn't have time to take you fishing."

"Oh, I don't know. Maybe after I get some of my chores finished, we could take a day to go fishing."

"Yippee!!" Katie cried, jumping up. "I'm finished with my snack, Mommy. Can I skip some more stones?"

"Just a few more—and don't get your tennis shoes wet. We need to leave soon."

While her daughter ran off, Abby said, "Sorry. When she's enthusiastic about something, she wants to do it. But you shouldn't offer to take her places if you don't intend to. She has the memory of an elephant when it comes to something she wants. She'll ask and ask each time she sees you, and be disappointed when it never happens."

"I'll have you know, ma'am," he said, his expression a little affronted, "I never offer something unless I intend to follow through. Especially not a treat to a child."

"Oh," she said weakly. "I . . . I didn't mean to question your sincerity. But so often people say—"

"Not me. Besides, you'll be at the cabin often. I'm sure on some occasion or other, we'll find time to take her fishing. How's your casting technique?"

"About as experienced as my wading technique," she answered wryly. "In fact, I've never been fishing."

"Never been—" He broke off, genuine shock on his face. "Darlin', you did spend too many years in the city! Time you were introduced to one of the river's delights."

Wandering back from her exploration of the wildflowers bordering the bend in the river, Katie said, "Can we go fishing soon?"

"Pretty soon. I've got more hay to cut and then I need to move some of the herd into other pastures, but after that, I should have some time in the morning. It's better to go early, while it's still cool. There are still a lot of bugs that got trapped on the river surface during the night, so the fish are biting. Sometime," he added with a glance, "on the weekend, when your mommy isn't working."

"Mommy works every day and every night after I go to bed," Katie told him. "In the daytime, she lets me draw and paint in her shop while she works."

"I thought ranchers worked every day too," Abby said.

He nodded. "They do. Cattle don't understand the concept of weekends. We'll have to arrange something that fits both our schedules, then."

"Speaking of schedules, I'd better get things packed up now. It's already going to be after bedtime by the time we get home."

Though Katie initially protested, Abby could see after a long day and the excitement of wading and skipping rocks, her daughter was tired. After a token resistance, Katie helped Grant and Abby pack up the remains of the picnic.

As they started back up the hill, Abby noticed Katie beginning to lag. Before she could take the girl's hand, Grant said, "Tired, Princess?"

Katie stifled a yawn. "A little," she admitted.

"How about I give you a ride?" he asked, then came over

to swing her, squealing with delight, up on his shoulders.

"You'll hurt your neck, carrying her like that," Abby protested.

"Naw," he tossed back. "I used to carry an eighty-pound pack. This little gal weighs almost nothing."

The sun had already lowered, leaving the trail back up in shadow. By the time they reached the ridge, it was about to set, orange and rose and pink, behind the western hills. By unspoken accord, they stopped for a moment to admire the sunset.

"Yes, I can understand why you want to live up here," Abby said again. "Even if it is pretty far from town."

"Not all that far. And I spend most of my days on the ranch anyway. You know, that thing about cows and weekends." Pausing by her truck, he helped a sleepy Katie up into her car seat, then walked Abby back to the driver's side.

"She'll probably be asleep before we get home. That wade in the river will have to do for a bath."

"I hope I didn't tire her out too much."

Abby laughed. "Are you kidding? After skipping stones, and wading, and giving her a piggyback ride, you'll be heading her list of 'Favorite People in the World.'"

"I enjoyed it too. Thanks for letting me tag along."

"Thanks for letting us explore your river. I'd better go. I'll text you when I have the designs ready."

"I'll be looking forward to it. Drive safe."

"I will. Goodbye, Grant."

"Bye, Abby. Talk to you soon."

Strangely reluctant to leave—it must be the incredible beauty of the site, Abby told herself—she started the engine and put the truck into gear. Grant gave her a wave, then walked back toward the front of the cabin.

The visit had gone far better than she'd hoped, Abby thought, encouraged. Though she'd never quite been able to ignore the low level hum of attraction between them, she'd been able to subdue it enough to feel more comfortable around him.

Of course, the fact that he'd respected—mostly—her previously stated intention to keep their relationship businesslike had helped with the comfort level. And his appreciation and indulgence of her darling daughter certainly boosted him up the likeability scale.

What mother could resist a man who had cheerfully spent nearly an hour skipping stones with her child?

She knew he and his younger brother were still bachelors, and his older brother was recently married. Maybe he had cousins or friends with young children, because he certainly was good with them.

All in all, after tonight, she was even more enthusiastic about beginning the project. And no longer quite so opposed to spending more time around Grant McAllister.

# Chapter Six

IN THE LATE afternoon three days later, a freshly showered Grant hopped into his truck and headed for Abby's shop. After she'd texted that she had some designs and samples to show him, they'd arranged to meet after he finished his daily chores.

He had to admit he was looking forward to seeing her again, and not just because he was eager to see her plans for the cabin. How could a man not like a lady who was very easy on the eyes, loved his Hill Country homeland, and had an adorable daughter? She might be city-raised, but she seemed to appreciate country things like wading in a stream, skipping rocks, and sharing a simple picnic snack beside a pristine run of river. Unlike so many urban professionals, she'd seemed not at all in a hurry, quite ready to adjust her pace to the lazy flow of the river.

He really liked that about her.

All of which reinforced his hope that eventually she'd agree to spending more time together, beyond just consulting on furnishing the cabin. But he would take it easy. After that complete shutdown when he suggested dinner that day at her showroom, she'd gradually relaxed as they toured the cabin and then spent time by the river.

And based on the times he'd caught her looking at him, he knew the simmering attraction he felt was mutual.

But there had also been unmistakable grief in her voice when she spoke about the husband she'd lost—even after five years. Grant hadn't known Ross very well, but he must have been quite a guy to have inspired such devotion.

Maybe Abby Rogers was a woman with the grit and loyalty to stick around for the long haul, through good times and bad.

Not that he was looking for anything permanent now. He was still finding his way with being back in Whiskey River and cycling his work with the veterans' organization to part-time. But compatible companionship was always welcome. He could look forward with anticipation to riding the ranch with her, maybe teaching her and her little sprite of a daughter how to fish.

No need to force anything. He'd follow her lead, adjust their interaction to the pace she was comfortable with, and see what developed.

He turned into the drive leading to her house, then parked in front. Since it was past office hours, he went first to the house. When no one answered his knock, he walked over to the showroom and rapped on that door.

"Abby, are you there? It's Grant."

"Coming!" she called from inside.

A moment later, she opened the door, and Grant's heart did another of those dizzying swoops. This time, she'd exchanged jeans for a loose, cotton sundress in a vivid blue green that brought out the deep blue of her eyes and the honey-gold hue of her hair. The sleeveless dress revealed shapely, tanned arms and legs, and though it wasn't tight, it still clung nicely in all the right places. If he were to draw a picture of the feminine physical characteristics that most appealed to him, the sketch would look just like Abby Rogers.

After trading greetings and a bit of small talk about the day, which allowed him to get his breathing regulated and his mind refocused, she said, "If you'll come over to the dining table, I've assembled some photos of things I thought you might like, along with sketches of how I envision the cabin."

"Willingly."

"Would you like coffee or water?"

"Don't happen to have any of that lemonade Katie makes, would you?"

She smiled. "As it happens, I do. Katie and Jillee made a fresh batch today."

"Shall I wait and we can share it with her after we're done?"

"She's not here. Jillee took her on to Marge's. I'm meeting them all for dinner later."

He must be making progress, Grant thought, if she felt

comfortable enough to meet him without any backup nearby to intercede if she felt uneasy. He would have to be careful not to do anything to jeopardize that advance.

"You spend a lot of time with Marge and Jillee, don't you?" he asked as they walked to the table. "I don't know Jillee, but I remember Marge from high school as being fun and adventurous."

"I don't know about adventurous, but she's still fun, and we all have daughters. The old hens and the young ones. Jillee's husband is a long-haul trucker, so he's gone a lot. With all of us living on a shoestring, a while back we started the Friday Night Club. We couldn't afford to hire sitters and go out to celebrate the end of the workweek, so we began staying in with the girls, letting them watch movies while we drank wine and talked. If one of us needed to run errands, or if Jillee wanted to have a weekend getaway with her husband in San Antonio or Dallas, the others watch the girls. Now that Marge is divorced, we get together more often. It's good to have friends to spend time with."

"Yes. It's always good to have friends. Which is why I'm looking to make more. As I think I mentioned, most of the people I graduated high school with have married or moved on. Aside from my brothers, I don't really have any friends here now."

"You moved back just to help Duncan out on the ranch?"

Grant nodded. "After Harrison's daddy died, she took

over the Scott ranch, but then the ranch's foreman got injured. My brother and some of the other ranchers pitched in to help her out, but with the spreads combined, now they need another hand on a more permanent basis. I can still work part-time with my old firm remotely, so when Duncan asked, I was happy to agree."

"So you think you'll be here permanently now?"

Grant smiled. "Like so many kids, I was eager to get away and check out the green of other pastures. I enjoyed bouncing around from place to place. But after a few years, I found that the place that suited me best, the place that held my heart, was here. This is . . . *home.* So yes, I guess I'll be here permanently. Which is why I'm willing to spend the time and money to make the cabin over just the way I want it."

"You said you still worked part-time with a firm? What do you do?"

"Getting out of the Marines . . . was a tough transition." Grant paused, pushing back the searing memories that time and training had allowed him to conquer—most of the time. "After healing and counseling, when I finally made it through, I wanted to help other vets with the process. So I started working with a firm that specializes in finding them jobs."

"At least you made it out. Now, shall we get started?"

"I'm ready," he agreed—noting once again how his mention of the Marines had erased the smile from her face and prompted her immediately to change the topic of conversation. No more mention of his time in the Corps, then.

He took the seat at the table she indicated, while she went into a small office in the back and brought back two tall glasses of lemonade. Taking his, he took a long, deep drink.

"Wow, that is good. Really refreshing after a long, hot day out in the pastures."

"Glad you enjoy it. Shall we look at the sketches first? And then I'll show you photographs of the sort of pieces I'll be looking to obtain or create."

He was pleased that she took the chair beside his—and supremely conscious of her close beside him. With a light, fresh scent of roses and woman filling his nostrils, he had to force himself to concentrate on the sketches she pulled out of a portfolio.

"The dimensions are approximate, but from what you described, I'd see the main entrance on the east side, the door flanked by the enlarged windows," she said, all business now. "On the north side, the fireplace, also flanked by windows. An oversize leather sofa and several chairs arranged in front of the fireplace, with end tables, a rug, and coffee table. On the other, south side, of the entrance, a long dining table and eight chairs. To the west of that, an eight-foot island with sink, dishwasher, and storage, with the fridge and stove on the west wall. Did I capture your vision correctly?"

"Yes," he said, nodding at the design. "That's how I see it."

"Do you like the style of leather sofa here in the showroom?"

"Very much."

"How about color?"

"That saddle tan is good."

She nodded. "There are several things we could do for end tables and coffee tables. I can just make something from objects I find on my next run through the antique and 'junktique' stores. Or I could fashion tables with storage using various sizes of galvanized water troughs for the base, like these."

After flipping through the photos, he pointed out one. "I like that for a coffee table. Maybe found objects for the end tables."

"Would you want the wood finished or painted?"

"I'd rather not have a mishmash of lots of different wood colors and finishes, so I'd prefer them all to coordinate. Lighter wood, rather than darker. A painted accent piece or two would be fine."

"How will your window frames be finished? Plain aluminum, or painted? There's a lot of black-painted metal being used now, which looks masculine, and contrasts well with the pale silver gold of Hill Country limestone."

"I like the idea of black contrasting with the stone."

"Are you going to use a gas insert for the fireplace?"

"Yes, I'll convert the wood-burning one. Not a lot of firewood available here, and I'd like to use the fireplace as one of the major sources of heat in the winter."

"Then you could install a black unit to match the windows. Other accent pieces could pick up the black. The water-trough bases for the tables can be painted black as well."

"I like that."

"I've included some photos of dining tables. Everything from old farmhouse to straight-line modern. Chairs from traditional ladder-back to mid-century to modern."

Grant flipped through more photos, pulling out the ones he liked. After which they discussed material for the island—she suggested facing the bar-seating side with limestone to match the cabin walls, an idea he liked—and then reviewed photos of cabinet designs and colors.

"Cast-iron beds for the bedrooms, right? What about the bathroom? Will you want a claw-foot tub, or just a shower?"

"I prefer showers myself, but it probably wouldn't hurt to have a tub as well. It's helpful to have a place to soak if a mama cow objects to you handling her baby, or a horse bucks a little too hard. Not claw foot, though. Something modern, and mounted against the wall, so it's easy to clean."

She smiled at that. "Will you do your own cleaning? I sorta thought you'd get a cleaning service."

"I might, depending on how well the ranch does. Might not be enough income for fripperies like that. One thing the

Marines teach you is how to clean a compartment."

Once again, her smile faded and he kicked himself for not remembering to avoid mentioning the service. She wouldn't be the first widow to blame the Corps for the loss of her husband.

Before he could divert her with another answer, she gave her head a shake, as if to rid it of whatever memory he'd inadvertently summoned up. "Yes, I can imagine. I can gather some bath and shower designs to show you once you are closer to finishing that space. How about the sink and vanity? I've done some using old farm sinks set into cabinetry, like this."

Relieved that she'd retreated only briefly, he warned himself not to slip up again.

"I like that one," he said, pointing out an old farm sink set into a sleek rectangular cabinet.

She nodded. "I'll be on the lookout for some farm sinks. I think that covers most of the main areas. What might work best is for me to text you pictures of the objects when I find them. If you approve, I'll buy them and bring them back to work on. I'd prefer to assemble all the various pieces first, then finish them together so that the look is cohesive."

"Sounds reasonable. I should pay you something upfront, then, to cover the objects you find."

She nodded. "If you want to advance a sum, I'd be grateful. Helps prevent cash flow problems."

"Growing up on a ranch, I know all about cash flow

problems," he said ruefully.

"I think it would be better to assemble all the major piec-es first, then look for finishing items—lights, artwork, fixtures, cabinet hardware to coordinate with them. And leave the details—linens, cooking items, silverware, rugs—until the very end."

"Sounds good to me. There are a few things I already know I want, though. A Texas map made out of roofing tin, like the one on the wall there. Several of those ladder book-shelves. I like the black-iron lanterns on the wall too."

Nodding, she made a note. "I'll put those down as defi-nite. I can look for several sizes and shapes of lanterns to paint black. That would tie in with the stove finishing and the window frames." Putting down her pen, she looked back up at him, grinning. "This is going to be so much fun!"

He laughed, beyond delighted with her enthusiasm. "Glad I'm giving you a project you can enjoy."

"I'm going to—immensely!"

"We've made a good start. I'd like to suggest, though, that you come on that ride around the ranch with me. So you can kind of get into your head the colors and textures of the land surrounding the cabin. When you start looking for linens and rugs and things, I'd like them to bring in those colors."

Abby went silent—and Grant held his breath. Would she agree to ride with him? Or had her earlier agreement been a throwaway line, a casual comment to deflect him from pursuing the matter rather than a statement of intent?

All he knew was he was more eager to give her that tour now than he'd been the day of the picnic.

Finally, after a hesitation that had his heartbeat accelerating, she said, "It will be . . . all business, right?"

"Of course. That's what you requested and that's what I promised. I honor my promises."

She stared at him a moment, as if assessing the validity of that statement. Fortunately, she seemed to believe it, for she nodded. "Getting a good feel for colors and textures would be helpful. Just be advised, I haven't been on horseback in a long time."

"Even after living in Whiskey River for almost five years?"

She laughed. "Yes, but I've spent most of that time with family. Marge grew up in the Barrels, remember, not on a fancy ranch. They didn't have the money to keep horses or learn to ride."

"I grew up on a ranch, but I can promise you, it wasn't fancy. We didn't have much money either, but in the early days, we used horses to work the cattle. We didn't get a work truck until I was in junior high. When finances got really tight, it was the truck or the horses, and the truck was cheaper. Harrison's daddy loved horses, though, and always kept several. The one Harrison likes to ride is just the mount for you. Gentle, easy-paced, and we'll do no faster than a walk." He put his hand on his heart. "That's another promise."

"Okay, I think I could handle that. When do you want to ride? Late afternoon, after you've finished the ranch work for the day?"

"It would be better for the horses to go early in the morning, when it's cooler. It stays hot pretty much until dark now."

"I could go on one of the mornings that Jillee comes to watch Katie—a Monday, Wednesday or Friday."

"How about this Friday? That will give you two days to arrange things with Jillee, and I can set up my work schedule accordingly."

"Won't riding in the morning set you back, so you'll have to finish work at the hottest part of the day?"

Grant shrugged. "I don't cut hay until after the morning dew burns off, and the tractor cab has air-conditioning."

"Okay. I don't remember anything on the books for Friday, but give me a minute to check my schedule."

He made a "go ahead" gesture, then waited as she pulled out her phone and checked her calendar. "Yes, Friday will work. What time?"

"Why don't you meet me at the Scott ranch at eight? The barn is just adjacent to the house. Or is that too early?"

She gave him a look. "I'm the mother of a five-year-old. If I want any quiet time, I have to get up with the dawn, before she wakes up."

"Okay, eight o'clock. I'll have water packed in the saddle

bags, so you don't need to bring extra."

She sighed. "What have I gotten myself into? Remember, I'll need the closest thing to a slug you have in the stable."

Grant laughed. "You'll be fine. Harrison's Snowflake is the sweetest, gentlest mare going. She'll take good care of you. And so will I."

"Right, saddle bronc rider. My preferred pace will probably bore you to death."

"There's a time for covering territory, and a time for slowing down to just appreciate the land. Like that picnic by the river."

"Well, if you can promise a leisurely pace like that, I guess I will manage to stay in the saddle for the whole of the ride."

"I'll make sure of it. Can't lose my designer before she even gets started on the cabin."

"Okay. Until Friday. I may take Katie and drive down toward New Braunfels tomorrow, to check out several places I've found pieces before. If I turn up anything I think you might like, I'll text you a picture."

"Great. If I don't answer right away, that'll mean I'm out in a pasture somewhere with no cell coverage. In that case, if you like it, buy it. From everything I've seen here in the showroom, I'll like it too."

She nodded. "I'll do that. If you decide you don't want something, I can probably sell it to someone else."

He clapped a hand to his chest. "Not something you envisioned for my cabin!"

"Getting possessive, when you haven't even seen anything yet?"

Looking at her sweet, sassy smile, he could see himself getting possessive. It would be all too easy to want to keep not just her designs, but the lady, all to himself.

Which was going way too far, way too fast, especially since she hadn't yet even committed to "friends."

Back off, cowboy, he silently advised himself.

She stood, signaling an end to the conference. Despite the sound advice he'd just given himself, Grant really wished he could ask if she'd join him for dinner—he would love to spend more time with her. But it would probably jeopardize the progress they'd made if he offered a suggestion that sounded more like a date than a business rendezvous.

Besides, she was meeting the girls for dinner tonight anyway.

He felt a wave of uncharacteristic emotion that must be . . . loneliness. There were definite drawbacks to having your only good friend in the area be your newlywed brother. Not a good idea to drop in unannounced on Duncan for dinner.

Maybe he'd drive into town and eat at the Diner.

He'd always been happy enough with his own company, if there weren't any friends around. Before. What was it about being with Abby Rogers that made him melancholy not to be able to keep the evening going?

Shaking off the feeling, he said, "Can I take the glasses back to the house for you?"

"No, thanks, I've got them." Bringing over a tray, she placed the glasses on it and pulled out a key.

Grant walked out with her, waited while she locked up the showroom, then walked her back to her front door, surprised at how strong the desire was to stay with her longer.

"Thanks again for agreeing to take on the project. I think the place is going to end up a masterpiece."

"If it does, I'll want to take pictures of it to post on my Instagram account, if that's okay with you. It might help me get more whole-house jobs, which would be great for building my business. Thanks again. For trusting me with your cabin."

He lingered on the doorstep, wishing he dared take her hand. And she lingered, too, not immediately bidding him goodbye and going into the house.

For a long moment, they both just stood there, gazing at each other. In her wide-eyed, wondering look, Grant read uncertainty, caution—and attraction.

What he really wanted was to kiss her. But that would be guaranteed to destroy all the progress he'd made.

Finally, with a sigh, she looked away. "Well, goodbye then. I'll see you Friday."

"Goodbye, Abby. Tell Katie I loved her special lemonade."

She smiled. "I'll do that."

This time, she did open the door and go inside. Grant walked back to his truck and climbed in. After sitting there a moment, he sighed, started the engine, and put the truck in gear.

He hadn't dared pull her into his arms today—even though he read longing as well as caution in her gaze. But somehow, someday, he knew he just had to kiss her.

# Chapter Seven

J UST AFTER DAWN two days later, Grant took his cup of
coffee out onto the back porch of the Scott ranch house. It
had been Harrison and her daddy's favorite spot for breakfast, his brother's wife had told him. Especially in the late
spring, when bluebonnets covered the broad meadow that
descended in a leisurely curve to yet another bend in the
river. Even without the wildflowers, with the sunrise to the
east painting the hills with pink, rose and purple, it was a
serene and beautiful spot.

Although he was naturally an early riser, he hadn't needed to get up quite this soon. But knowing Abby would be
meeting him today, once he'd awakened just before dawn, he
hadn't been able to go back to sleep.

He really did need to rein in his eagerness to see her—
although he wasn't sure how to go about controlling what
had been his immediate, instinctive response to her. An
attraction that spending more time with her had only
intensified.

But he'd promised her to keep their relationship "all
business." Unless and until she gave him an indication that

she was ready for something more—expressed in words whose meaning was unmistakable—he would have to abide by that promise.

Meeting on horseback today would be fortunate for several reasons. He could show her the ranch he loved—and not have to fight with himself to keep his distance.

He wouldn't have enough time to go out to the pastures to check on cattle and get back before she was due to arrive, but he could log on to his computer and check his business email, see if any matches had come up to employment searches for the several clients he was managing, and answer any queries they might have sent.

Putting his mind to solving other vets' problems would keep him from thinking about his own—how to entice one irresistible lady to take a chance on a relationship with him.

Finishing his coffee, he gave the countryside one more appreciative scan and headed back inside.

After a scan of his email revealed that he had employment offers for two of his clients, he spent the next hour calling each of them, explaining what the jobs entailed and encouraging them to apply. He felt especially driven to persuade the second, an Army vet who'd lost both legs below the knee and who was having a hard time dealing with the loss of his strong, physically intact body, to agree to interview for the position as a personal trainer.

"You were the squadron trainer, Rafe," he told the client. "Nobody knows more about how to exercise and which exercises to do to strengthen each muscle group. It'll keep you in the gym so you can work on your own fitness program. Maybe build up to running that veterans' 10K race next fall."

He held his breath, hoping he hadn't pushed too hard, but after a long pause, Rafe said, "Okay, maybe you're right. Maybe having a goal like that will keep me working hard. It would be easier to train if I'm already at the gym, for sure."

"It helped me when I was rehabbing," Grant said. "I'm giving you my highest recommendation to the gym manager, so do me proud, won't you?"

"I'll give it my best shot."

"That's all I ask. You'll let me know how the interview goes?"

"Sure thing. And . . . thanks, Grant."

"No problem, buddy. That's what I'm here for."

Punching off his phone, Grant felt a sense of satisfaction tempered by lingering grief. Bleeding, his left arm shattered, he'd had to leave his buddies dying on that ridge when they medivacked him out. He hadn't been able to save them.

But each time he helped a vet, the guilt of surviving when they hadn't eased just a bit.

TWO HOURS LATER, Grant was finishing up in the barn, his horse and the docile one he'd chosen for Abby tacked up and ready, when he heard her truck approaching up the drive. A thrill of excitement and anticipation energized him. "All business" or not, he knew he was going to enjoy spending the morning in her company.

Leading the two horses, he walked out and waved, then tied the reins of their mounts to the paddock fence while she drove over to park next to the barn. A moment later, Abby jumped down, sensibly attired in jeans—which he would have preferred to be a tad tighter—and a long-sleeved shirt. She reached back inside to grab gloves, jacket, a backpack and a hat off the seat before shutting the door.

"I don't have proper riding boots. I hope these will be okay," she said, gesturing down to what looked like leather winter boots.

"As long as you're not in high heels, you'll be fine."

She laughed. "I haven't worn high heels in so long, I'd be a danger to myself walking down a sidewalk, much less riding. Is this my gentle mount?" she asked, gesturing to the smaller horse.

"It is. Abby, meet Snowflake. She's a perfect lady, just like her rider."

Abby reached into her jacket pocket. "I hope she likes apple." She offered the mare the treat and, nickering, the horse accepted it, stripping it delicately out of her hand.

"That's a smart way to get on good terms with her," Grant said approvingly. Maybe she knew more about horses than she'd let on.

Abby nodded. "I thought we'd spend a few minutes getting acquainted before the ride. Why 'Snowflake,' by the way? Doesn't snow much here."

"Harrison's daddy was a career Navy man. His last duty station before buying the ranch and moving here was up north. Harrison said the white blaze on the mare's forehead reminded her of a snowflake."

"Does Snowflake like to have her head stroked?"

"She especially likes having her neck rubbed."

Nodding, Abby stepped closer, talking softly to the mare while rubbing her neck. After few minutes, Snowflake nuzzled her shoulder.

"I think she likes you."

"Good. I like her too. And what is your big boy named?"

"This is Lightfoot. Harrison's daddy named him that because he seemed to pick up his feet so daintily, like he was almost trying to tiptoe. But what he really loves is to gallop."

"I hope you've told him there will be none of that while I'm along today."

"He's been informed and took the news with good grace. Are you ready to head out, then?"

Abby took a deep breath. "I guess so. I'm hoping after she ate my apple, Snowflake would feel guilty if she unseated me."

Grant laughed. "Very little chance of her unseating you today. She's well-trained and fully accustomed to all the terrain on the ranch. We won't encounter anything she hasn't seen before, nothing that might spook her or make her shy."

"I only hope I won't," Abby said wryly.

"Nope. There'll be only delights on the ride today."

"Is that another promise?"

"You bet."

He watched while Abby put her foot in the stirrup and swung herself up. Once she was positioned, reins in hand, Grant mounted his gelding. Turning back to Abby, he said, "Would you feel more comfortable if I took the reins and led her, while you get used to the saddle?"

"No, I think I can handle her. Just don't go galloping off and leave me. Now, where to first?"

"We're heading for the highest ridge on the property. It offers the best vista in three counties."

"Better than the cabin?"

"Even better than the cabin."

"The view must be pretty spectacular."

"It is. On a flat plateau reached by trails from either side of the ranch. It was our favorite camping spot when my brothers and I were growing up. Duncan, especially, was devastated when we were forced the sell off the parcel of land that includes it. Brice and I both moved away after high school, so its loss didn't bother us as much, but we're all still grateful to have it back again. Now, in case you ever wondered how I spend most of my days, we'll be riding past several of the meadows I've recently mowed."

"You just start at one fence and keep going until you reach the other, right?"

Grant laughed. "It used to be that simple, back when I was cutting hay for my daddy. But not anymore. Duncan studied all about it when he was at Texas A & M and had to train me."

"How could cutting grass be complicated?"

"Ah, it's not the cutting, it's the kind of grass. The ag scientists have extensively studied all parts of the cattle business over the last twenty years, with the goal of producing the largest number of the healthiest cattle. Since grass is one of their primary food sources, the scientists studied grass types and tested them to determine when they reached their optimum nutritional value, so they could be cut just at the right time to make the best possible feed."

"How do you decide when it's right? You can't just ask the grass if it's ready."

"No. It varies for the different grasses. Bermuda grass is cut according to a time schedule, others like Johnson grass or sorghum-type hays are cut at a certain stage of maturity. Some grasses can be cut twice, some up to six times a season. So you aren't able to just cut a field and be done with it for the year."

"Sounds like a lot of work."

"It is. But it's work in the open air, in beautiful countryside that it's a pleasure to spend time in."

"What sort of grass is that?" Abby asked, pointing toward

the field they were passing.

"That one is Bermuda. I've cut it once already; it will be ready for a second cut in a few weeks."

Abby shook her head. "You're right. It's way more complicated than I imagined."

They'd reached the point where a narrower trail branched off from the ranch road, curving up and down before rising steeply up to the plateau he'd described. Where he'd camped, not so very long ago.

"We take the side branch here—heading for up there." He pointed to the ridge in the distance. "It's too narrow to ride side by side, and it's pretty steep in some places, but Snowflake knows the trail well. Just hang on tight. She'll follow Lightfoot. If you feel like you're getting into difficulty, give a holler."

Abby gave the rising trail a dubious look. "I'll do my best to stay in the saddle."

"I think you'll be fine. I only mentioned it so you wouldn't be alarmed when the trail gets narrower and steeper."

As he'd expected, they both reached the plateau without trouble. Once they'd crested the last rise and arrived at the flat ground, Abby gave a whistle.

"Wow and *wow*! I didn't really believe there could be a view better than the one at the cabin, but you're right—this is. Can we dismount for a while? I'd like to take some pictures."

"Sure. Might be a good time to drink some of the water I brought. Easy to get dehydrated out in the sun, even early in the day."

Dismounting quickly, he walked over to take the reins while Abby slid down from the saddle. When her feet hit the ground, as he'd suspected might happen, her knees buckled.

He grabbed her arms to keep her from falling, steadying her against his body—guiltily aware that he was enjoying this opportunity to touch her, hold her. Looking startled and a little alarmed, she gazed up into his face.

Her eyes were the most incredible deep blue under improbably long lashes. Her skin flawless, with a faint dusting of freckles, her nose perfect—and her lips perfectly kissable.

He steeled himself to remain motionless, not crowding her space, forbidding himself to lean down and steal the kiss he wanted to so much. As soon as she regained her balance and tried to step away, he reluctantly let her go.

"S-sorry!"

"No need for apologies. Your legs can go out on you sometimes when you dismount after not having been in the saddle for a while. By the time we finish the ride today, you should be acclimated again."

Despite his reassurance, her face colored. Looking away, she pulled her phone from her pocket and slipped the backpack off her back. "I'll take some photos, and if we can spare the time, do a few color patches. The photos will show the panorama, the height of the hills and valleys, the textures. But the camera often doesn't capture the same color the eyes see. I prefer to use pastels to remind me of the exact hues."

"Sketch and photo away. I'll get us some water."

Grant led the horses over to a leaning cypress tree near a patch of rough grass and secured the reins, then pulled two bottles of water from his saddlebag. Leaving the horses to graze, he walked back and handed Abby a bottle.

After taking a long drink, she handed it back. Curious about her process, Grant trailed along as she drifted around the plateau, snapping pictures, then pausing to select the appropriate pastel stick and color a square on her sketchpad.

After ten minutes of wandering, she put the phone back in her pocket and beckoned him to come look at the sketchpad.

"I think I have all I need. The gray-green of the live oak leaves, the tan-gray of their trunks and branches. The sable-tan of the dried grasses, the tan-white edged with gray of the limestone bedrock. The varying greens of the trees on the far hills and the deeper greens and blues made by the shadows of the clouds. The brighter blue of the sky. That will give me a good palette of colors to work with."

"Sounds perfect to me," he thought, envisioning his cabin filled with soft, Hill Country hues.

After she stowed the sketchpad in the backpack, Grant offered her the water again. "Let's finish this up, then ride toward the McAllister ranch house. There's an old barn there. It mostly houses a collection of old gear we don't use anymore, but you might find something you can use."

"Old gear?" she repeated, her eyes lighting up. "I'll almost certainly find some things I can use."

He walked her back to the horses and stood beside Snowflake while she remounted—just in case her knee buckled and she lost her balance again. Unfortunately, her legs had recovered, robbing him of a perfectly acceptable excuse to touch her again.

After swinging back into the saddle, he waved a hand. "We'll head back this way. The trail to the ranch road on this side is much shorter, so you shouldn't run into any trouble."

A few minutes later, they reached a well-traveled dirt road that linked the pastures and led back west toward the McAllister house and barns. As they rode past several meadows, Abby asked, and Grant, pleased by her interest, identified the kind of grass being grown in the fields.

"Where are the cows, by the way?" she asked after they'd passed several empty enclosures.

"We move them around from pasture to pasture so they don't overgraze any of the fields. As it gets drier in the summer, we leave the cows in the areas closest to the river, where the topsoil and the grass are thicker. The herd's split into smaller groups now, since the bulls are still in with the cows."

"Aren't they always?" Abby asked with surprise.

"Do you know anything about cattle ranching?"

"Not a thing," she confirmed.

"Okay. Just wanted to make sure I wasn't telling you something you already knew. After the spring branding, when we vaccinate all the new calves and check the cows who didn't calve, we put all the cows out to pasture with the herd bulls for about a month and a half, then pull the bulls out and pasture them by themselves for the rest of the year. That gives us a controlled calving season from late winter into spring, rather than having calves drop all year long."

"Ah, yes. I can understand wanting to concentrate the work into separate seasons."

"We may see Harrison on our way back. She likes to drive or ride out and check on the bulls. Her daddy turned his part of the ranch into a seed stock operation, the purpose being to breed and raise the bulls and cows that produce the best offspring. Rather than selling them for beef production, he raised his cattle to sell to other cattlemen, to improve the bloodlines of their herds. Whereas the Triple A has always raised cattle solely for the beef market, selling them off either after weaning or after they reach market weight, depending on the going price of cattle for one market or the other. Now that the two ranches have merged back into one, we're keeping both operations going. Harrison's daddy was very fond of his bulls. He named them all and visited them almost daily. Used to feed them out of his hand."

"A full-grown bull?" Abby asked. "Aren't they rather—

dangerous?"

"You're probably picturing a charging bull and a matador. The Spanish breed their bulls to be fierce and aggressive, but those are definitely not traits you want in bulls destined to become herd daddies. Mr. Scott prided himself on producing bulls with easygoing personalities and docile temperaments, as well as good body weight and exceptional virility. Harrison said they used to come running to the fence when her daddy rode up, then followed him around the pasture, nudging him with their heads, coaxing him to give them more feed. They do remember and get attached to people. Harrison's trying to establish the same sort of relationship with them her daddy had. She thinks having a thousand-pound bull nuzzle your shoulder is sweet."

Abby shuddered. "'Sweet?' I'd call it 'scary!' More power to her, but I don't think I'd trust a thousand-pound bull, no matter how docile the breeding book said he was supposed to be."

Grant nodded. "I have to admit, I don't turn my back on them either."

As it turned out, they didn't encounter his sister-in-law before Grant and Abby reached the old barn. Reining in, he pointed down the road. "The new barn is down there, closer to the ranch house. Easier to access in bad weather, which is when we do a lot of the maintenance work on the equipment and vehicles."

"So this barn contains all the bits and pieces that aren't

used any longer?"

"That's right. If I'm remembering correctly, I think there's some old tin roofing in there we could use to make one of those Texas maps. And who knows what else."

"Perfect! It will be like a treasure hunt!" Smiling with delight, Abby slid from the saddle—keeping a hand on the pommel this time until she was certain her legs would support her. "You're right. This dismount was easier."

"Go on in. I'll take the horses to the water trough for a drink and then meet you."

"Okay. Can't wait to see what I can turn up."

WHEN GRANT JOINED her half an hour later, he had to smile. Her eyes bright, her expression excited, Abby was rummaging through a stack of old milk cans, her shirt and jeans covered with dust and a smudge of dirt on her cheek.

"This is great!" she exclaimed. "I'm like a kid in a candy shop."

"More like a kid in a mud puddle," he corrected, reaching up before he thought about it to brush the dirt off her cheek.

Silently cursing himself, he held his breath, but after going rigid for a moment, Abby simply moved out of arm's reach. Apparently choosing to ignore the gesture rather than reprimand it, she said, "What I've found is worth a little dirt.

Come see!"

Relieved that his impulsive touch hadn't spooked her, he followed as she led him into what had been one of the barn's stalls. Stacked against the wall were several galvanized milk jugs, an ancient, leather, plow-horse harness, wooden crates of assorted sizes, a couple of old rakes with broken handles, a windmill with two badly bent blades, and a box full of old branding irons.

"The milk jugs can be painted black, wired, and turned into sconces—for lights on the porch or in the bedroom hallway. I've seen the plow harness made into a mirror frame, the wooden crates can be stacked into an open-form cabinet or dresser, and the rake heads will hold wineglasses, like the ones in the buffet in the showroom. If I can bend the blades back flat without breaking them, the windmill pieces can be fashioned into a clock. But I'm especially excited by these!" she finished, gesturing at the box of branding irons. "Can I really take these? You don't use them anymore?"

"Yes, you can take them. That's the old style of the Triple A brand. Duncan redesigned it when he took over the ranch after college, using brands made of a metal alloy that lasts better than the old iron ones. Though a lot of times we don't brand at all anymore, we just use the ear tags."

"I haven't made one yet myself, but I've seen pictures of branding irons used to create a chandelier. You construct two rings of iron, one smaller at the top, one larger at the bottom, and hang the brands from them, with LED lights strung on the top edge of the iron rings, and up and down the irons, too, if you like. You can use more or less lights depending on how much illumination you want the fixture to provide. Rather than make a cedar-root chandelier to hang by your fireplace, how about I make the fixture out of these? The black iron would echo the black metal edging the windows, the feeding-trough table bases, and the lanterns. Plus, it would display something of the history of the Triple A in the cabin your grandfather built. Of course, if you didn't like it after I got it finished, I could just hang it in the showroom and make you the cedar-root one you asked for."

Something more of his heritage to display in the cabin that was his inheritance? She really did understand what he valued. Not just the colors, but the character of what he put into his home. He was gladder than ever that he'd asked her to furnish it.

"Sold. I love the idea. And I bet I'll love the finished product too."

"Great! Now, you said there might be some old tin roofing somewhere?"

"Yes, I'm pretty sure there is. Have some more water while I locate it."

Grant handed her another bottle of water, then went off to the far side of the barn to look for the slabs of roofing tin. Pleased to find them where he remembered seeing them, he selected two likely sized candidates and dragged them back to lean against the barn wall along with the other items Abby had collected.

"Looks like you made a pretty good haul. I have to admit, I wasn't sure there would be anything useful here except for the roofing tin."

"No, it's been a bonanza! I have some other projects to complete first, but I can't wait to get started on all of this."

"I'll load them up in the truck and bring them by your workshop later. By the way, speaking of 'sold,' I wrote you a check. It's back at the Scott ranch house. Make sure I give it to you before you drive home. As down payment for your work and prepayment for whatever objects you end up buying on your collecting trips."

"Thanks, that will be helpful." Finishing off the water in the bottle, she said, "We'd better head back now. It will take us some time to ride at the leisurely pace I prefer. Katie will be waiting on me for lunch, and I have some projects due soon I need to work on this afternoon."

Stifling an automatic protest—he'd enjoyed the morning with her so much and wasn't ready for it to end—Grant nodded. "I should get the tractor ready and mow the next meadow. It's one of our larger ones—will probably take me until dark to finish it."

Together they walked out of the barn and down the road to fetch the horses Grant had left in the paddock. He retrieved their watered and rested mounts, stood by while Abby climbed into the saddle, then remounted his gelding.

"Thank you for inviting me to ride today," she said as

he—reluctantly—guided Lightfoot onto the farm road leading back to the Scott ranch house. "The ranch is beautiful. I can see why you felt called to come back. Though I've only lived here five years, this area has become special to me too. A place to heal. A place where, with the help of Ross's family, I was able to find myself again."

"I had to find myself again before I could come back," he surprised himself by saying. "After my last tour—but sorry, I've noticed you don't like hearing about anything to do with the service. Subject closed."

She smiled sadly. "I don't really blame the Marines for losing Ross. It was his choice. His choice to deploy again, even after he knew I was expecting Katie. Mentioning the service does bring back memories of a hard, sad time. Memories I thought I'd finally worked through. Guess I haven't been as successful at that as I imagined."

"Memories aren't so easy to escape—especially the ones you'd rather forget."

*Like pain . . . and loss . . . and the agony of not being able to save your buddies,* he thought, knowing he would always have to work to keep some of them at bay.

"Losing Ross brought me to his family—and this place. I'd always done craft projects growing up—much to my mother's dismay. Nothing but products made by top brand-name manufacturers was good enough for her. She was . . . ashamed of the objects I made and wouldn't allow them to be displayed outside my bedroom. Used to tell me if I'd spend half as much time on clothes and makeup as I did pasting together trash, I might look halfway decent for a change."

"Wow. That's pretty harsh!" He might never meet Abby's mother, but he already disliked her. No wonder after Ross's death, Abby had chosen to take refuge with his family rather than her own.

She shrugged. "That's my 'Mommy Dearest.' But maybe it's good we never got along. If I'd gone back to Dallas instead of bringing Katie here, I might never have attempted larger projects. Never discovered the work I do now, which I love. And need to get back to this afternoon!"

"What are you working on now?" he asked, as willing as she was to turn the conversation to less-painful topics. Even though he was gratified that she'd shared something personal with him.

That had to mean she trusted him more now, didn't it?

"Lately, it's been teacups." She chuckled. "I made a pink-teacup lamp for Katie's room and posted pictures of it on my Instagram feed. It's turned out to be one of the most popular items I make—that particular lamp and various versions of it. I've become the teacup queen. I buy up all the teacups I can find at secondhand shops and junk stores and have the owners of several places holding them for me whenever they acquire some."

"I can picture a single teacup lamp, but I'm having a hard time envisioning anything else."

"Oh, there are lots of variations. You can halve the tea-cups and mount a series of them against a wall, like sconces. Put a hole in the bottom and hang them upside down as pendants, with or without their saucers. Hang them from several rings of increasing size to make a chandelier. Stack several of them together, with or without saucers, as a lamp base. Or stack them on top of teapots, if you want a larger base for a table or floor lamp."

Grant shook his head. "Who knew?"

"All sorts of kitchen objects can be made into lampshades. Colanders, painted any color the client wants. Square, metal cheese graters. I'm making some kitchen island pendants for a client now using pastry blenders with little lights inside them."

"I'd like to see your workshop. Maybe I could come by some afternoon and help you make the Texas map picture. Or at least see how you do it. I don't want to disturb the artist while she's creating."

"Maybe," she replied noncommittally.

She might not want anyone invading her private place. But at least she hadn't turned him down flat.

"By the way, I'll feeling pretty confident on Snowflake now. If you want to let Lightfoot have a little run before he goes back to the paddock, go ahead."

"He does like a run, but that can wait for later. It wouldn't be polite to leave a guest. Even though it would be hard to get lost—you just follow this road until you come to the barn."

"I might even try a trot."

"Great. Give Snowflake a nudge with your heels; she'll be happy to comply."

Flashing him a smile, Abby signaled her horse to change gaits. Snowflake immediately went to a trot. Grant followed, although he had to curb Lightfoot, who really did want to gallop.

Moving at the faster pace, they reached the barn a short time later. As they reined in, Abby looked to him with a smile. "That really was fun. I remember liking horses, but I didn't particularly enjoy riding."

"Ah, but you weren't riding Snowflake then. I'm glad you enjoyed it—and hope you won't be too sore tomorrow! Takes time to develop saddle muscles."

"Can I help you put up the horses?"

"No, it's almost lunchtime, so you'll need to get back. I'll leave them in the paddock and get that check for you."

She dismounted with more confidence this time. "I'll chat with Snowflake while you get it."

So much for her following him into the house, maybe getting her to linger for a glass of water. Good thing she had Katie waiting for her, else he might be tempted to invite her to stay for lunch.

But it had been a great ride, so he wouldn't be greedy enough to wish for more—this time.

After snagging the check off his desk, he walked back out

and handed it to her.

"Thanks. And thanks again for the ride. It really was the best way to see the ranch."

"We'll have to do it again sometime. Maybe figure out a way to bring Katie."

"That would be dangerous! After being on a horse, she'd never want to go back to riding in a car seat again. And *please* don't tell her about petting bulls!"

"When would you like me to bring over the things from the barn?"

"Text me first, but I should be available pretty much any afternoon. You can drive them over after you finish work for the day. Well, I'd better get back."

"The teacups await?"

"The teacups await. And Katie, of course."

"Tell her I'll be looking forward to a glass of her lemonade when I drive over. If that's okay with you."

"Fine. But just to warn you, she'll probably ask about fishing."

Grant chuckled. "I'll look on my work sheet before I come and figure out what would be a good time to take her."

"I should be able to start on some of your items next week, after I finish my current order. I'll want to drive by a few places and look for the furniture items—and anything else that seems promising—first. I'll let you know when I have everything assembled, and you can drop by. I'll tell you what I'm envisioning making, and you can let me know whether or not you like the ideas."

"Sounds like a plan. I'll see you in a day or so, then."

"Great." Abby opened her truck door to stow her items inside, then climbed up. "See you, Grant."

"You, too, Abby."

Grant gave her a wave, which she returned after she'd backed out. Then watched as she headed off down the gravel drive.

He'd be eager to see what she accumulated, and her vision for what she'd turn the items in to. He'd be even more eager to see her again.

Walking back to the paddock to tend to the horses, he thought again of how she'd shared a bit more about how she came to Whiskey River. Even as he had hinted a bit about the long road that had finally led him home.

That put them on the path to being friends, didn't it?

Though opening up about his own journey was hard to do without mentioning the military, a topic that apparently brought back such negative memories, he really didn't want to upset her by discussing it.

Which was okay. He'd rather encourage her to talk about herself, her daughter and her work anyway.

Maybe next time they met, he could risk asking her to spend time with him on something that wasn't strictly "business-related."

# Chapter Eight

I N THE LATE afternoon several days later, Abby was in her workshop, putting the finishing touches on another teacup lamp, when her phone dinged a text message alert. Glancing over, she saw it was from Grant, asking if it would be convenient for him to bring by this afternoon the items she'd found in the barn.

Hesitating to reply, she blew out a breath. She was excited to get the objects in hand and start working on them. She was not so excited about seeing Grant McAllister again.

Because reading that text and thinking about him coming by had sent an immediate surge of gladness through her. And she wasn't sure she was ready to allow herself to start liking any man that much.

She was being ridiculous, she told herself stoutly. Okay, so she was attracted to him. But nothing needed to come of it unless she later decided she wanted it. He'd respected her space, just as he'd promised. After that one instance when he'd asked her to dinner the first time they met at her showroom, he'd given no further indications he wanted her to be anything more than the interior designer who furnished his cabin. If he'd wanted to get fresh, he could easily have stolen a kiss that time he caught her after her knees buckled getting down from the saddle.

Did she want him to kiss her?

She sighed. The attraction might be unwanted, but she was too honest to deny the strength of it. Held close to him when he'd steadied her on her feet, looking up at his face, she had been almost—mesmerized. Those deep blue eyes. The strong jawline, the lean, tanned face. That aura of competence, strength—and kindness.

It made her want to trust him, to offer him the friendship he said he was hoping to find in Whiskey River.

Marge said he was one of the good guys.

But maybe that was a good reason not to let him get too close. It would be too easy to fall for a good guy who also attracted her, a combination she hadn't run into since Ross. She didn't want to, couldn't *afford* to, fall for anyone with the intensity she'd loved Ross.

It had taken her too many long, painful years to dig herself out of the abyss of despair and loneliness after his death. Too many years to escape the sense of helplessness her mother had so successfully instilled in her and gradually reinvent herself into the person she was today. An independent, talented woman confident in her abilities, able to support herself and her child. A woman intent on building a business whose expansion remained her one goal and priority, outside her daughter.

If she hadn't had a baby to protect and care for, she might not have been able to struggle free of her mother's damning assessment of her worth.

But she did have Katie, and the love and affection of her child was more than enough to meet her emotional needs, just as her business was more than enough to fill up her days—and nights. Katie's love was steady and steadfast, a constant Abby would never lose, and her business, a rock to keep her centered.

And then she had to laugh. Unsettled by her unexpected, unwanted, but instinctive, response to Grant McAllister, she was making this into something much more serious than it was. All Grant had mentioned wanting was friendship. If he should be looking for an affair, she had a daughter to tend to, to keep her from succumbing to that temptation.

He was almost certainly no more interested in something more intimate than friendship than she was.

He'd only been back in Whiskey River a short time. A handsome, well-spoken, *nice* guy like Grant wasn't going to lack for feminine company very long, once he made it known he was available. And there was sure to be a ready supply of fish willing to bite on a passionate, short-term hookup, if he wanted that.

Hadn't Marge said the girls in town were already atwitter?

It was only normal to respond to a kind, handsome man. She'd learn to manage the attraction better. To be the designer he wanted rather than the woman he didn't need her to be. To be the successful designer *she* needed to be.

Perhaps, if she were cautious, maybe also a friend. But nothing more.

Picking her phone up, she texted him back that it would be fine for him to bring the things by today.

JILLEE HAD GONE home and she was sitting outside with Katie, drinking lemonade, when Abby saw Grant's truck approaching down the county road. Katie saw it, too, exclaiming, "Look, Mommy! It's Mr. Grant!"

"You remember I told you I'd found some things in Mr. Grant's barn? He's bringing them to Mommy's workshop. I'm going to make them into lamps and dressers and things for his cabin."

"Will he tell me when we can go fishing?"

"He might. But if he doesn't, it wouldn't be polite to ask him about it. He has a lot of work, taking care of his cows and horses and mowing the meadows. If you ask him and he's too busy to do it now, he'll feel bad when he has to say no."

Katie thought a minute. "I wouldn't want to make him feel bad. I like cows and horses, Mommy."

Wanting to head off the probable direction of that re-mark, Abby said, "I do, too, Katie-girl, but they are a lot of work and we don't have a place to keep them."

"Can we go visit Mr. Grant's cows and horses some-time?"

"Maybe. You can go inside and color while I help him carry the things into the workshop, or you can come with us if you want. Just be careful. Some of the objects have sharp edges. We're going to store them in the back, and I don't want you to touch them, okay?"

"Okay. I want to come to the shop with you, but I'll be careful, Mommy."

A few minutes later, Grant pulled up his truck in front of the showroom. As he climbed down, Abby gritted her teeth at the zing of attraction that zipped through her.

*You'll get used to it*, she told herself. *Once you've started consulting with him regularly as a client, the feeling will fade.*

Katie skipped over to meet him. "Hi, Mr. Grant! Mommy said I can't ask you about going fishing, but I still want to go."

While Abby rolled her eyes, Grant laughed. "I might be able to find some time next week, Princess. Do you want to help me and your mommy carry some things into her workshop?"

Katie nodded. "I like to help. Mommy says I can't touch anything sharp, though."

"That's a smart idea. You think you could get me some lemonade first? I need to carry in two big pieces of tin, which are very sharp and also very bendy."

He looked up from Katie to Abby, who had just reached the truck. Once again, their gazes met and held. Her mind went blank, and for a moment, she just stood there, staring at him.

"Hi, Abby," he said at last, jolting her out of her trance.

"Hi, Grant," she said, feeling her face flush at having stood there gaping like the village idiot. "Thanks for bringing everything over . . . and for asking Katie to fix lemonade while you carry in the tin."

"Why don't you help her? It will keep both of you out of harm's way. Tin has a mind of its own. It might buckle on me while I'm carrying it, and I don't want anyone getting hurt."

"Probably a good idea. Let me go open the shop door for you. Katie, will you go into the house and get another glass for Mr. Grant?"

After hurrying ahead to prop open the shop door, she said, "Put the tin against the far wall, behind the gated area. Katie often comes into the shop while I'm working, so I keep the dangerous stuff over there, where she can't accidentally get into it."

Wrestling with the first sheet of tin, Grant nodded. Giving him and the unwieldy sheet a wide berth, Abby walked back to the café table and helped Katie pour a fresh glass of lemonade for each of them and garnish them with mint leaves.

Grant emerged from the shop a few minutes later and

walked back to his truck to pull out and carry in the second sheet of roofing.

As he came back out the second time, Katie called, "Your lemonade is ready, Mr. Grant."

"Thanks, Princess. Let me take off these gloves and I'll be right there."

Gloves in hand, he walked over to take a seat beside Katie. Although seated on Katie's other side, Abby was all too conscious of his physical presence. He radiated a calm competence and a heady masculinity that kept doing odd things to her breathing.

*You'll get used to it*, she told herself again.

"You do make the best lemonade," Grant was telling Katie.

Her daughter nodded solemnly. "I'm a good helper. I can help you carry things to the shop too."

"I bet you can. I'm sure you are a big help to your mommy."

For a few more minutes while they sipped their drinks, he chatted easily with Katie, asking her about her latest drawings and the favorite games she liked to play with her cousin, Sissie. Once they'd finished the lemonade, he led them back to the truck, where they unloaded the objects Abby had chosen.

She noticed he was careful to evaluate each item, making sure the ones he handed Katie weren't too heavy and didn't have any sharp edges. While they carried them in, Grant played a game with the girl, asking her to guess what each object was used for.

Katie easily identified the wooden crates and rakes. For the other items, she shook her head, not certain enough to hazard a guess.

Handing her one of the galvanized metal milking jugs, Grant said, "Do you think we could use it for lemonade?"

Katie shook her head. "No, it's too big."

"How about putting flowers in it?"

Katie looked at it doubtfully. "It would need a lot of flowers."

"How about for milking cows? When my brothers and I were growing up, the ranch kept milk cows. We would milk by hand and pour the milk into these big containers."

Katie's eyes widened. "Really? You put cow's milk in these?"

"We did." Hefting the bladed top of the windmill, which he'd removed from the base, he said, "What about this?"

"It looks like a fan, but it's too big."

"It's sort of like a fan. The blades are bent now, but if they were straight, they would turn around."

"Like a pinwheel? Mommy got me a pinwheel at the fair once."

"It's just like a pinwheel. When the wind moves the blades, a lever attached to them operates a pump that brings water up from the well into a trough for the cows and the horses. Now, what about this?" he asked, holding up the last item, the old horse collar. "Do you think it might be a hair bow?"

Katie giggled. "No, it's much too big."

"A boat?"

"It doesn't have a bottom! It would sink!"

"A bicycle tire?"

By now, Abby was laughing, too, at his suggestions as her daughter squealed a "no!"

"What is it used for, Mr. Grant?"

"When my grandfather was little, the ranch didn't have tractors. They used plow horses to till up the fields and seed hay for the meadows. This is the collar they put around the work horse's neck, to spread out the weight so it didn't hurt him when he pulled the heavy plows."

Katie shifted her gaze from Grant to Abby. "Mommy, how are you going to use a plow in Mr. Grant's cabin?"

"The leather collar is oval and really stiff—it hardly bends at all. I'm going to put a back on it and then put glass on top of that to turn it into a mirror."

Sighing, Katie looked back at Grant. "My mommy makes the most wonderful things."

Grant chuckled. "So I've observed. I can't wait to see what she will do with all the things we've carried into the workshop."

Katie nodded solemnly. "She'll make them beautiful, just like my teacup lamp."

"I'm counting on it."

Once all the items had been stowed away in the workshop, Abby said, "Shall we wash off our dusty hands and have some lemonade? I think there's just enough left for each of us to have another glass."

Meeting with universal approval for that suggestion, they washed up at the workshop sink, then walked back out to the terrace. "Katie and I are going to go exploring soon to look for dressers, farm sinks, side tables, and anything else that looks interesting."

"Collecting teacups as you go?" Grant asked.

"Definitely teacups, if there are any to be had."

"Are you coming with us, Mr. Grant?"

Alarmed, before Grant could reply, Abby quickly inserted, "Mr. Grant has to work on his ranch, Katie. Cows and horses need to be fed and watered and tended every day. You can't just go off and leave them. But he's going to come back to the workshop later and look at all the things we've picked out."

"If you help your mommy pick them out, I know they will be special."

Katie nodded with the precocious seriousness five-year-olds sometimes display. "They have to be special. Your cabin is a special place."

"I certainly think so."

By now, they'd finished off the lemonade—and it was getting close to dinnertime. Knowing he lived alone and had few friends in the area, Abby was tempted to ask Grant to stay and join them. But it wouldn't be a good idea to set that precedent, even if it did make her feel guilty to send him away hungry after he'd helped her out, transporting all the items for her.

But if she wasn't going to invite him, she'd better get him to leave before Katie did—which she very likely would, if dinner was mentioned. There would be no gracious way to circumvent an invitation then.

So, setting down her glass, Abby stood, signaling the end of refreshment time. "Thanks for bringing everything by and saving me a trip."

"You've welcome," Grant said, rising as well. "I figure you'll be wrangling that roofing tin soon enough. You didn't need to fight it to get it over here too."

"I should start working on your items soon, probably day after tomorrow, if I get the rest of the teacup lamps finished. There will be more to see after Katie and I make our shopping run."

"Including the Texas map?"

When she nodded, he said, "Would it be possible for me to come by and help—or at least observe? I'm really intrigued to see how you do it. I know I asked you once already, and I don't mean to be pushy about it. But I like crafting things, and I'm thinking I might try making some other items with the tin. Maybe a map of the county or the ranch."

Closing her lips against an unexpected urge to immediately agree, Abby hesitated.

It wasn't that the prospect of being observed made her uncomfortable. Katie often accompanied her into the workshop, drawing, coloring, or playing with games or dolls on a little table Abby had set up for her while she crafted items whose component parts wouldn't be dangerous to a curious five-year-old.

But could she concentrate on her task, if *Grant* were standing close by, observing? A little shiver went through her at the thought.

On the other hand, she knew how much she enjoyed turning odd bits and pieces into useful, attractive objects. It would be satisfying to tutor someone truly interested in that creative process, equipping him to do other projects by himself.

And she was a grown woman. It was time to stop running away from the response he fired in her, meet it head-on, and subdue it.

"I don't want to crowd you or distract you," he added as she remained silent. "I won't be offended if you'd rather not."

"No—you wouldn't crowd me." Which was probably a lie, but she had to start somewhere if she wanted to turn it into the truth. "I was just figuring when would be the best time to work on it. Probably Saturday. I prefer not to have Katie in the shop if I'm going to be cutting glass or tin or using welding gear, and she'll be at Marge's then. You're welcome to stop by, if you're sure you have the time."

"I can make time for that map. When do you think you'll start working?"

"Marge is picking Katie up at noon. The girls are going to see the new Disney movie in town."

"I bet you'll love that, won't you, Princess?" Grant said, turning to Katie.

"Yes! It'll be so much fun. 'Specially cause Sissie and Meghan and I get to sit together."

Silence fell for a moment. Before Abby could head off Katie—who, by the expression on her face, *was* about to issue Grant a dinner invitation—Grant said, "I'd better get going. It's almost dark, and I need to check on a few cows in the south pasture."

"Can I go see your cows sometime, Mr. Grant?"

"Sure, Princess. Maybe we can take a tour of the ranch the day we go fishing. If your mommy says it's okay."

"Yeah, fishing!" Katie cried, jumping up in delight. "I love cows. And horses. Mommy said she rode a horse named Snowflake."

"She did. You could meet her, if you like."

"Could I ride her too?"

"I'm afraid she's a little too big for you. But you could climb up on the fence, rub her neck, and feed her an apple."

"Oh, Mommy, can I?"

"Later. If Mr. Grant says it's okay. But you mustn't tease him about it."

"I won't!" Katie promised. "I'll be very polite."

"Why don't you go inside and wash your hands for supper while I walk Mr. Grant to his truck? If we finish dinner in time, we might be able to watch a movie before bedtime."

"Yeah!" Katie said again. "I'll be ready right away, Mommy! Bye, Mr. Grant!"

"Bye, Princess," Grant called after her as she skipped to the house, singing "Movie, movie, movie!"

Abby walked with Grant to his truck—just as conscious of his nearness and its potent appeal as she'd been while she and Katie sat beside him on the love seat.

So much for becoming accustomed. But she'd make strides on that this Saturday, she promised herself. "Thanks again for bringing everything over."

"My pleasure."

Abby reined her thoughts in before her long-denied senses could create a different image to match those words. "I'll see you Saturday, then."

He nodded. "Yes. Saturday, noon."

Giving him a wave, she watched him drive off and then walked slowly back to the house.

Was agreeing to let him work with her Saturday a mistake, dooming her to an uncomfortable, frayed-nerve afternoon as she was pulled between attraction and the need to resist? Or would assuming a teacher's role to guide him through a process she thoroughly enjoyed provide the transition she needed to move from an acute consciousness of his physical appeal—and her needy response to it—to accepting that attraction as normal and unthreatening, something she could move beyond, maybe into friendship?

Sighing, she opened the door and headed in to dinner.

It was too late to back out now. She'd just have to answer that question on Saturday.

# Chapter Nine

J UST BEFORE NOON Saturday, Abby stood on the patio, waving goodbye as Katie drove off with Marge. It was a measure of her daughter's excitement about seeing the new movie that she was still eager to go, even though she knew Grant, who'd quickly become one of her favorite people, would be coming to the workshop.

Frowning, she watched Marge's SUV disappear into the distance. Though she was pleased Grant was so good to Katie, she didn't really want her daughter getting too attached to someone who was only going to be around on a temporary basis. Advice she needed to heed herself, before she started becoming too fond of his company too.

For the last three days, she'd struggled with the same back-and-forth, want-to-be-friends, shouldn't-risk-being-friends feelings she'd had after first agreeing to work with him today. But though the idea of him coming by still sent butterflies fluttering around her stomach, she repeated to herself the conclusion she kept coming back to.

Grant McAllister was a client, and as such, she would need to consult with him a number of times while she worked on furnishing his home. She'd be meeting him both at the workshop and at his cabin as items were crafted and as she experimented with placing them. If she couldn't resolve the discomfort of being around him, she would have to renege on her agreement and turn down the commission.

And she really shouldn't turn down this opportunity to create a complete houseful of furnishings—which could be such a fantastic springboard to advance her business.

Which meant she had to master her reaction to him, and the sooner, the better.

Not only would that permit her to work with him without the prickly unease she now felt, it would be nice to savor, just a little bit, being around a handsome, virile male who was as easy on the eyes as he was kind to her daughter.

As long as the experience didn't make her pine to have someone like him around on a more permanent basis. She already knew how distracting handsome, compelling Grant McAllister could be, and she didn't have time for distractions.

She'd need to master her nervousness quickly too. Tin roofing was a potentially dangerous material. Become inattentive, and she could easily slice open a hand or a finger—which would be disastrous. She'd not be able to keep up with the orders she needed to fill and work on Grant's project with one hand out of commission.

That sobering fact ought to keep her focused on the task.

The sound of a truck approaching down the county road

sent a little shock to her nerves. *Grant.* Putting a hand on her stomach, she willed the butterflies to cease fluttering.

*He's a good guy—and he doesn't want to make you uncomfortable. A good guy who happens to be handsome and appealing. Yes, it's been a long time, but you can handle this.*

Then he was pulling up, shutting off the engine, and climbing down from the truck.

*Showtime.* Taking a deep breath, she walked over to meet him.

"TWELVE NOON ON the dot. Are you always so punctual?"

"Time is valuable and always in short supply. I didn't want to keep you waiting. Did Katie get off okay?"

"Yes. So excited we could barely persuade her to fasten her seat belt, she kept jumping around so."

Grant smiled. "Sorry I missed it. One of the things I love about kids—they are so open and honest about what they like—or don't like."

"You sure are good with them! You must have friends or relatives with kids."

"One of my best buddies in the service. Since I was single, he and his wife used to invite me home for dinner pretty often. They had a cute little girl like Katie, and an older boy who loved to arm wrestle and play football. It reminded me a lot of when I was growing up with my brothers."

"Were you close?" Abby asked as she walked with him to the workshop.

"Very. Near to each other in age, and nearly inseparable. Of course, we spent most of the time we weren't in school helping Daddy run the ranch. With no other kids living anywhere close, when we had time to cut up or play around, it was generally just the three of us. So I guess it's good we got along well."

"You still see them often."

"Duncan pretty much every day, since we consult about ranch business. Brice, not as much. He's a Texas Ranger and often travels to work on cases. He's based in Austin, though, so he tries to get by when he's working out of the home office."

"You must enjoy being back home and spending time with them again."

"I do. The Corps is a brotherhood, too, but nothing beats brothers of the blood."

*She knew all about the strength of that brotherhood*, Abby thought, pulling her mind away before her thoughts could turn bitter.

After unlocking the shop door, she led Grant inside. "Shall we get started?"

"Can't wait. I brought heavy work gloves, by the way. Wasn't sure you'd have any large enough to fit me."

"We'll work back in the gated area."

He was following her, but halted as they were passing

Katie's table—an old end table to which she'd added a drawer, some colorful paint and scrollwork. "This is cute, but awfully short. Designed for children?"

"It's Katie's. On the days when Jillee isn't watching her, she likes to be nearby, so I made her, her own 'workbench.' That's why I put up the gate—so I could isolate her from the saws, tin snips, welding gear, and other stuff that could be hazardous. Unless I'm really pressed on a deadline for an order, I reserve doing projects that need those tools for when Jillee is watching her, and work on less dangerous or complicated projects when she's in here with me. Even if the tools I'm using aren't hazardous, a five-year-old's attention span isn't very long. I'd rather not be halfway through putting together something intricate and have to stop to help her with something."

"I can understand that."

"Speaking of complicated and intricate, are you sure you can spare the time to help me with this? I imagine it's pretty hard to fit in working on the cabin after doing all your ranch chores."

"It is, but fortunately, it's the right time of year for multitasking. The sun comes up early, so I can check on the cattle before it's dry enough to begin the mowing. Then it stays light late enough that I have time to work at the cabin after the ranch chores are finished."

"Makes for an awfully long day."

He nodded. "True, but watching the cabin come back to

life is so satisfying, it's worth it. All I need to do when I think about skipping a day is envision what it's going to be like, sitting out on the terrace watching the sun go down, the gold ribbon of river below me, nothing but orange-and-crimson sky to the west, as I sip a beer and savor the smell of steak grilling for supper. That always inspires me to keep going."

"It does sound pretty wonderful," she admitted. "It's a beautiful setting, and once it's finished, will be a beautiful home."

"I'll have to have you and Katie over for steak after everything is finished." Maybe he saw alarm flare in her eyes, for he quickly added, "I can have Duncan and Harrison join us too. I think you'd get along well with Harrison. Another independent, determined woman. Although her talent is with numbers—she's an accountant. She'd just gone off to college when her daddy bought the ranch. After she inherited it, she decided to leave the city and settle here for good."

"Sounds wise as well as talented. I'd enjoy meeting her—and your brother, of course. So how's the work on the cabin progressing?" she asked as she pulled out assorted tin snips, markers, cardboard and pattern pieces.

"It's going well. The stonemason's been out and we got all the windows cut. After the plumbing was roughed in, my general contractor had his crew pour the foundation for the addition, then after the concrete cured, sent them back to frame it. The roof will be going on in the next day or so. I was going to sheetrock the place myself, but I think I'll let the contractor's team handle that and put my time in on the finishing work. Once the subfloor is in, I can start putting down flooring and putting up the shiplap on the walls in the bedroom. Will have to wait until the kitchen island and cabinets are in to do the floors in the old part of the cabin."

"You are making progress," Abby said, impressed.

"I'm pleased with it so far."

"I'll be looking forward to seeing it again."

"I can't wait to show it to you—and see your designs in it."

For a moment, he held her eyes with the force of his gaze. Instead of jerking her head away, Abby made herself look steadily back. Acknowledging the pull she felt to him, rather than trying to ignore it. Admitting that she felt it, telling herself she *could* feel it without being threatened.

Ross had been her whole world. But now she had Katie and her business. She could be attracted to a man without losing herself completely, as she had when she'd lost him. She was her own person now, and she was stronger and more independent every day.

Liking Grant McAllister could . . . complement, rather than threaten the life she'd rebuilt. Her physical response to him didn't have to distract her from her goals or interfere with running her business.

Desire fizzed in her blood, danced in her nerve endings. It was still a bit scary, dizzying almost . . . but the panicky sense that she needed to run in the opposite direction faded.

So pleased by that progress, she just barely kept herself from grinning—how would she explain that idiotic response?—she instead said, "I'm eager to place my designs in it. Which should be the signal for us to get working. If you would go get the smaller piece of tin, I'll move these lamps out of harm's way."

"Some of your teacup lamps, I see."

"Yes."

He paused for a minute, studying them. "Clever. Very delicate and feminine, though. I hope you aren't envisioning one for my bedrooms."

"I thought it would be a fine fixture for the master bedroom." At his look of alarm, she held up a hand, laughing. "Just teasing. Most of my orders for these are for little girls' bedrooms, or ladies' dressing rooms. Although the halved teacups on this bench—the solid-color jade and milk glass and pink depression glass ones—make striking sconces along a hallway or a wall in an avant-guard or mid-century modern décor. The glass just glows when you place a light inside."

"How do you make them without breaking the cups? They must be pretty fragile."

"It's not complicated. You do have to be careful, because porcelain and glass are delicate. Drilling the hole to begin the cut is the hardest part. Mostly, you need patience; if you try to drill through it too fast, or apply too much pressure, it's likely to split or crack. Once you have the hole cut, halving it, or putting a lamp together is easy. A lamp kit from the hardware store takes care of the wiring, and there are lots of options to use for the column and the base, depending on how feminine or fancy you want to make it. Gold, brass- or silver metal, PVC, hollowed-out wood."

He walked over to the bench and picked up another item. "This is to make one of those colander lights you talked about?"

"Yes. A client wants a set painted blue to hang over a kitchen island."

He shook his head. "Who would have thought?"

"Lots of items can be repurposed to new uses. Just like people moving on to new lives."

"A widow becoming an inventor-designer?" he suggested.

Is that how he saw her? Pleased, she said, "Or a cowboy turned builder?"

"We can all learn and move on."

"Yes. How else would we survive?" That comment skirting too close to painful truth, she said, "Ready to start on the tin?"

"Absolutely."

"Okay. While I get my template, would you put the tin up on the workbench?"

After donning his gloves, he centered the tin, then helped her clamp it into place. After handing him goggles and a dust mask, she placed her cardboard template on top of the tin.

"I use some sticky putty to hold the template in place—

any of the products that can attach posters to a wall will work. Then trace around it with a Sharpie, like this," she said, demonstrating. "Once I have a good outline, the template comes off and the cutting begins."

"You use old-fashioned tin snips, rather than power sheers or a circular saw?"

"Yes. A circular saw would really only be useful if you were cutting a lot of tin in straight lines," she said as she carefully removed the template. "As for the power sheers, you'd have to be pretty good at moving them around and controlling their speed to accurately make all the bends and angles required for a map. Besides, when I was starting out, I couldn't afford fancy power tools. I picked up different sizes of tin snips for cheap at garage sales or farm tool sales."

She shook her head. "Too many of the latter. Ranching and farming, as you certainly know, is a tough business. In a lot of families, it seems the children of the owners either don't want to or can't afford to continue the business when the older generation dies or retires."

Grant grimaced. "Which is what happened to the Cameron place. The house you live in used to be occupied by the ranch foreman."

"Really? I didn't know. Now I feel guilty!"

"You shouldn't. If the place couldn't continue as a ranch, I'm sure the Camerons would much rather see a small business operating on the property, using the existing buildings, than having everything torn down and turned into fancy condos."

"Well, that makes me feel better," she said as she stowed the template back in a cabinet. "Now comes the part of this project that demands patience. The tin cuts more easily than I expected when I first started out. But controlling the curves and stopping the cut just where you need to can be tricky. Added to which, the tin, since you can't completely secure all sides of it while you're cutting, sometimes turns cantankerous and tries to escape."

Picking up the tool, she continued, "Since the first curve we need to cut goes counterclockwise, I'll start with the red-handled, left-handed snips. I use the yellow-handled ones if I have a long enough area where I can cut in a straight line, and switch to the green-handled, right-handed snips when I need to cut a curve that goes clockwise. Have you used tin snips before?"

"Back in the mists of the past, probably, when I was in high school. And only to cut in a straight line to size a replacement roof panel."

"Cutting in a curve is, once again, not difficult. Just takes patience and steady, consistent pressure against the tin."

While he stood nearby, watching closely, she continued to carefully cut the curving outline, explaining as she reached different areas some of the tricks that allowed her to change the angle without having to constantly change out snips.

Although she had to silently admit having him standing nearby still induced a flutter in her stomach and a heady awareness of his closeness, the necessity to concentrate on the work muted it to a tolerable level.

After about forty-five minutes, with a little more than half of the outline completed, Abby stopped and set down the sheers.

"Need a break?" Grant asked. "Your hands and shoulders must get tired, holding the tin steady and operating the sheers."

"It did when I first started doing these, but I'm pretty used to it by now. I thought maybe you would like to try cutting some."

"Are you sure? I'm a rank amateur. I wouldn't want to mess up your work."

"I don't think a cartographer will be dropping by later to grade the accuracy of the finished product."

He chuckled. "Probably not. Okay, I'll give it a try."

"I stopped before this section on purpose. The next bit of cutting is straight, so you can experiment and get the angle of the snips against the tin and the pressure right before you have to cut a curve."

She handed him the yellow snips, feeling a little tingle, despite their work gloves, when his fingers grazed hers. He looked up quickly before taking the snips—just long enough to let her know the jolt she'd felt had been mutual.

Oh, my. So Grant McAllister was as attracted to her as she was to him? She was going to have to be even more careful than she'd thought!

# Chapter Ten

KEEPING HIS ATTENTION on the tin, Grant inserted the snips where she'd left off and carefully extended the cut.

*All business*, Grant reminded himself. If he wanted to lure her into being friends, he'd have to keep a tight control over the attraction between them.

Slowly, carefully, he continued cutting, managing to follow her outline with surprisingly few errors.

"Do you want to finish it?" she asked after he'd cut around several curves.

"I would, if you don't think it will harm the finished product too much."

"Not at all. For your first time cutting curves, you're doing amazingly well."

Pleased by her praise, he looked up and grinned. "Thanks. I'm usually good at projects that take brute force—banging flooring in place, nailing up shiplap. This is my first time trying something that requires more finesse."

"I think you have the touch."

Turning his attention back to the tin, he said, "Do you

make other objects out of the tin roofing?"

"I've made stove hoods from it and used it as a back-splash in kitchens. You can use it like wainscoting in a room too. Use it instead of wood in lots of places—as a backing for bookcases or hutches or even headboards and footboards for a bed. Frame it with wood for garden planters. Cut it into decorative letters to mount on a wooden base. And it makes a cute roofing for all kinds of small projects—birdhouses, mailboxes. The possibilities are endless. Just have to make sure you sand off the sharp edges if you are using it for a decorative piece."

Her ingenuity was so amazing, he had to laugh. "Makes my idea of creating another map seem pretty unimaginative."

"Using it to make something that fits its setting makes it creative. Maps that connect to your land, your history, are wonderful bits of décor for a cabin built by your grandfather."

"Now *I* feel better. I do like the idea of personalizing the cabin with things that have meaning. Another of the incentives to keep going, no matter how tired I sometimes am. To have a place of my own, yet something connected to my family—on land my great-grandfather settled."

"It must be good to grow up in a place you feel you belong," she said, her tone wistful.

"Was Dallas not home for you?"

She shrugged, considering the question. "No. Not really. To be honest, I was sort of the odd duck in my family.

When I was a kid, sometimes I thought I must be a changeling. I never really felt like I belonged."

"Never belonged?" he repeated, surprised—and sad for her. "I'm sorry. I feel like our family was really lucky. After my mom died when Brice was born, my dad eventually remarried my mother's cousin. But she had been coming by to look after us for several years by then, and we already felt like a team. It's the worst possible thing, to have a problem at the heart of your family."

"I wouldn't know," she said wryly. "All I remember of growing up was problems. My handsome, dashing father, my elegant, beautiful mother, my elegant, beautiful older sister, and me—the ugly duckling in the swan's nest."

"You, an ugly duckling?" he exclaimed. "Now that I cannot believe."

She chuckled. "Okay, I've improved in looks since I was a kid. But growing up, I was chubby, with thin, dishwater-blond hair. My mother had been a professional model, and my older sister followed in her footsteps, beginning when she was still a child. Mother loved going to her photo shoots—and dragging me, pointing out how pretty and vivacious Ashley looked. By the time I got into high school, I'd started slimming down and my hair lightened up, but by then, it was too late. I was the awkward, shy, unaccomplished one who embarrassed my mother by disdaining makeup and fashionable clothes, going around in jeans and a sloppy sweatshirt, and spending my time working on tacky craft projects. The one who was never good enough or pretty enough."

"Why do people sometimes not appreciate you unless you value the same things? I was always grateful that Duncan didn't resent me or Brice for not wanting to stay in Whiskey River after high school and help him run the ranch."

"Hiding myself away and working on those craft projects eventually paid off. If I hadn't mastered a lot of basic techniques growing up, I would never have had the courage to attempt more complicated items—or ended up establishing the business I have now."

"Finding what you were meant to do—by hook or by crook." Despite the denigration she'd received from the people who should have loved her, he thought, aggrieved on her behalf.

"As you've found your way back to the Triple A?"

He was about to tell her more about that journey—then remembered what telling the story would entail. Rather than distress her and bring an end to these insights into her background he was finding so fascinating, he said, "I suppose. Speaking of the Triple A, how did a girl from Dallas hook up with a guy who, as far as I know, never left Whiskey River before he joined the service?"

Abby smiled. "Craft projects again. I had just graduated from high school, wasn't sure what I wanted to do next. I'd been making toys and dolls for a local homeless shelter, and the manager told me if I had extras, I should donate them to the Marine Corps Toys for Tots campaign. Ross was TAD in Dallas after he finished Marine Corps Basic and Infantry School and had been put in charge of the local drive. I met him when I brought in my dolls. He made such a big deal about how beautifully made they were! I think that's why I started falling for him. He was the first guy I'd ever met who seemed to value what I loved to do."

So she finally met someone with eyes and more than half a brain in his head, Grant thought. "I should think he would. You're incredibly talented. Besides, no girl can resist a guy dressed in Marine Corps blues."

"Well, my motives weren't so noble—at least, not at first," she said with that wry grin he found so enchanting. "After he chatted me up that first day, he asked me out. To be honest, one of the main reasons I accepted was I knew my parents would be horrified. The daughter of bank president Thomas Richardson, Dallas socialite Gwenneth Richardson, dating a Marine corporal from Podunk, Texas? And they *were* horrified. But by the end of that first date, I didn't care what they thought. He was so . . . attentive, and genuine, and fun, and . . . kind. Knowing he was a Marine, I'd armored myself to fight him off when he tried something. Instead, at the end of the evening, he walked me to my front door, kissed me on the forehead, and told me I was the loveliest, most special girl he'd ever met."

Grant listened closely, both wrapped up by her story . . . and a little bit jealous. At least the guy who'd recognized her worth had been a fellow Marine. "Kudos to him for being smart enough to see that."

She smiled wryly. "After that, I was a goner. Two months later, when he got orders to his permanent duty station, I told him I wanted to come with him. Being the old-fashioned gentleman he was, he said if I wanted to stay with him, I'd have to marry him. Despite how little time we ended up having, saying 'yes' was the smartest thing I've ever done."

"So he eventually charmed your family, then?" Grant guessed.

"No. They were awful to him. When I told my parents we were getting married, my mother told me to shack up with him if I wanted, but not to tie myself to a boy with only a high school education who hailed from a hick country town the other side of nowhere—and who was about to deploy to a combat zone. She added that if I did marry him, and he got himself killed, not to bother running back home to Dallas. So I didn't. Ross told me after we married that if . . ." She stopped and swallowed hard, as if pushing back a wave of grief.

Alarmed that speaking about her loss seemed to upset her so much, he was about to assure her she didn't need to say anymore when she took a shaky breath and continued. "He said if anything ever happened to him, I should come to Whiskey River, and his family would take care of me. And they did."

Thank heaven the Rogers family had been worthy of the name. "From that description of your home, you made the right choice coming here. I'm glad Ross's folks took care of you as they should. So you no longer have any contact with your own family?"

She sighed. "I didn't for a long time. But despite how bitter our parting was, after Katie was born, I got back in touch."

"You made the first move, of course," he said drily.

"I did," she admitted. "But my parents are her grandparents, after all, and I felt they should at least know about her, even if they chose to have nothing to do with her. Which they didn't until she was about three. I'd been sending them pictures and occasional cards, and all of a sudden, out of the blue, my mother showed up in Whiskey River and wanted to meet her. Of course, she was charmed."

"How could she not be? Your daughter's irresistible."

She smiled at that. "Thank you, kind sir! Certainly I think so! Katie is the beautiful, golden child I was not. I admit, I resent—a little—having my mother make such a fuss over her. She's always sending expensive presents or fancy dresses that simply aren't appropriate for a girl living in ranch country. And I really don't like that she buys so many toys and things for Katie when we visit." She blew out a sigh. "Sometimes I wish I hadn't gotten back in touch, but it wouldn't have been right not to let them know about their granddaughter."

"No matter how poorly they treated their daughter?" Grant said, having a hard time suppressing his anger.

"Not that things improved . . . much. When Mother visited the first time, I'd just opened the showroom. She walked around, looked at everything, then asked me when I was going to stock 'real' furnishings instead of logs, castoffs, and old kitchen gadgets."

Grant shook his head, beyond disgusted. "No wonder you don't want to see her. I suppose she thinks the only items that display good taste are those that appeal to her?"

"Of course. She has a superior education, was a highly sought-after professional model, and still moves at the highest level of Texas society, rubbing elbows with millionaires, mayors, and business leaders, sponsoring museum exhibits and gallery openings. People who like crafted things are lowbrow, uneducated rubes. Well, enough about me. Sorry! I'm not sure what got me started on this maudlin review of the past."

"Don't apologize, please! I wanted to know more about you. And it's okay to talk about the people you loved. Necessary, even if you lose them. Maybe especially if you lose them." Or so the therapist had counseled him. Might it help Abby to talk more about her losses?

But apparently she'd said all she intended, for she waved a hand before saying, "Was there no great love in your life?" When he hesitated, she said, "Come on. Turnabout is fair play. You've just heard the short version of my entire life."

She was right—and he should be pleased she was interested in knowing more about him. "There was someone special once," he admitted, setting down the tin snips. "While I was in the service. I thought she was 'the one.' But when things got rough . . ." He sighed. "I had one really bad tour. We lost a lot of guys. I was . . . pretty messed up and crazy when I got back. She couldn't deal with it. Just walked out while I was still doing therapy and rehabbing from my injuries. Brice and Duncan were there for me, though. Helped me work through it. I might not have made it without them."

"I'm sorry," she said softly. "Thank heaven for all the good families in Whiskey River."

"They're the best. You ended up in the right place."

"And you've ended this map in the right place!" she said, turning the conversation back to work. "Quite an impressive result for your first time cutting curves in tin. You said you'll be doing shiplap paneling in the bedrooms? I usually mount the map on shiplap. Do you want that as the backing, or some other material that won't repeat the wall treatment?"

"Shiplap will be great," he replied, accepting her return to more impersonal subjects—and glad she'd revealed as much as she had. "I plan to hang this in the main, stone-walled part of the cabin, so it won't be shiplap on shiplap."

"Okay, I'll finish it like that for you. And I should have the other pieces collected by the start of next week."

"You're taking the long-awaited shopping trip over the

weekend?"

"Yes, but as a sideline, not the main goal. I'm scheduled to take Katie to visit my family in Dallas this weekend."

"After what you've just told me, I'd guess you're not exactly excited about going."

"That would be an understatement," Abby said. "It's always a . . . strain, going back to Mother and Father's. Although we generally don't see much of Father. On the weekends, he's out playing golf with some corporate client or his country club friends. My sister is still modeling and relocated to New York recently for her career, so we usually don't see her, either. Coping with the full force of my mother's attention, trying to head off her attempts to make extravagant purchases for Katie without seeming too ungrateful, is a tricky balancing act. I'd much rather just stay here and hang out with Marge and the girls but . . ."

He wished he dared to talk her out of going away. Dared to maybe try to lure her into spending time out at the cabin, which she and Katie seemed to enjoy so much. But he shouldn't discourage her from doing what, however unpleasant, was right.

"I understand. Duty calls."

"It does."

"I really admire you for doing this for Katie, despite how little you enjoy the visits. Maybe your mother will eventually wise up and come to appreciate you."

"Right. And maybe the Blanco River will start flowing

west. But as long as Mother loves Katie and is good to her, it doesn't matter how she treats me."

He gave her a look that said he didn't quite believe that. It made him frustrated and furious to think of what she'd had to endure, still endured, from her sorry excuse for a family. He wished there was something more he could do to make her feel better.

Before he could come up with anything, she said, "When do you think you'll have the flooring finished? I should probably come out then."

Back to business once again. "I'm hoping by the middle of next week. At least for the floors in the new addition."

"Okay. I can refine my measurements and get a better idea of where to place the things I'll hopefully pick up on my Dallas run. And you can stop by the shop sometime later in the week and take a look at them before I do the final finishing, make sure they meet your approval."

"It's a deal. Do you want me to leave the map on the workbench?"

"Yes, please. I'll assemble the backing first, then fit it together."

"Will you need some help?" he asked, scrambling for an excuse to stay longer.

"Thanks, but I'm used to handling it myself."

"Going to pick up Katie now?"

"I'll work here a little longer first. I need to finish up the rest of the lamps. Then I'll drive into town."

He paused, watching her. Feeling the buzz and crackle of the attraction between them, hoping she might ask him to linger and share a glass of wine on the terrace.

When she remained silent, accepting the inevitable, Grant said, "I'd better be going then and let you get to it. So you're not too late picking up Katie. Thanks for the lesson. I think I will make a map of the Triple A to pair with the Texas one."

"If you have a county map with the boundaries marked, you can use tracing paper to create an outline, then cut it out and paste it onto cardboard to make a template."

"Or maybe bring the map to you and let you make the template?"

"Sure, I could do that. I should deduct the cost of the Texas map from your bill, since you provided both the tin and the labor."

"Consider it a training fee. So, I'll see you next week, I guess?" he asked, wishing it would be sooner.

"Yes. I'll text when I'm back. You can let me know when the floors are ready, and I'll come out to the cabin."

"Have a safe drive north, then. And as pleasant a visit as possible." *Or I might have to drive to Dallas and strangle your mother.*

She sighed. "I'll try—for Katie's sake. At least I can look forward to visiting the secondhand stores and junktique shops on the way back."

As she walked him to the door of the workshop, the

power of physical connection between them intensified. He looked down at her, intending to say goodbye, and lost his train of thought—lost it gazing into the depths of her blue, blue eyes.

Before he realized what he intended, he'd bent toward her. As her eyes widened—in alarm, probably—he caught himself, opened the door and quickly stepped outside. A cold sweat chilled desire as he realized how close he'd come to blowing all the progress he'd made by kissing her.

"See you, Abby. Say 'hi' to Princess for me."

"I w-will," she stuttered, looking as unsettled as he felt.

"Careful while you're working. Wouldn't want you to slip and cut anything important."

"I keep my cell phone at the ready in case of accidents."

"Just make sure you don't need to use it—not for that."

"Bye, Grant. Good luck with the flooring and the paneling."

"Thanks. Even if the cows and the hay cooperate, I'll still need it."

Desire still tingling along his nerves, he made himself walk to his truck without looking back. He needed a long, hot mowing session and the physical demands of pounding in flooring to cool his libido down—and figure out better ways to control the need she inspired in him.

Because learning more about her today had drawn him ever further under her spell. He didn't want to scare her away now by making any physical demands. He wasn't sure where his fascination would take him—but wherever that was, he knew he had to follow.

Whether it led them toward becoming friends, lovers— or something more.

# Chapter Eleven

B LOWING OUT AN unsteady breath, Abby watched Grant drive away. Wandering back into the workroom, she had to shake her head. Her body still had this humming, buzzing sensation going and her fingers tingled like she'd just gotten an electric shock.

She hadn't dared shake his hand goodbye. Just standing there, breathing in the subtle scent of aftershave and virile male, had made her senses clamor for something much more intimate.

If she felt that aroused just standing next to him, what would it be like to kiss him?

*Spectacular*, her senses whispered.

She had no trouble believing that. If she ever lost her way and touched him, she'd probably crave far more than a simple kiss. And she didn't need to even start down that road.

"Friends" would be difficult enough to manage. But she had made progress today, she reassured herself. Enough to allow an attempt at friendship, at least until her commission was complete.

But feeling more comfortable about that attraction and indulging it were two different matters. Succumbing to that temptation could lead straight to the distractions—and loss of time—she couldn't afford.

Because he was not only too attractive, he was too nice. Too easy to talk to. Having not had a handsome, kind, attentive man pay attention to her in so long, she could get carried away, especially after a glass of wine.

Carried away enough to kiss him.

And that wouldn't be fair, because it would give him an entirely erroneous idea of what she intended. Going all cold and distant afterward would make it seem like she was playing the tease, or blaming him.

Even worse, it would be all too easy to get too depend on him. She'd have to guard against that. She'd been oh-so-tempted to accept when he offered to help her mount the map onto its backing. Yes, mounting the map was a difficult, tricky and potentially dangerous process, but she'd done it numerous times by herself. She'd worked very hard to become self-reliant. She couldn't afford to let someone take over, take care of her, slipping back into having someone else make the decisions or do the hard things for her. Jeopardizing that hard-won independence.

Not when she had Katie to raise and protect.

Not when she was so close to achieving her dreams for the business she'd been working so hard to establish.

No matter how kind, attractive and helpful the man was.

It didn't help that Grant reminded her so much of Ross. Not physically—Grant was tall, his dark wavy hair worn a tad too long and his eyes a striking blue, whereas Ross had been shorter, more powerfully built, with a square jaw and dark eyes. Since he'd been a Marine with a regulation haircut the entire time she'd known him, she didn't know whether his sandy hair would curl or not.

But Grant had the same considerate, helpful, kind personality. The same quality Ross had of focusing his whole attention on her, listening like what she said or watching like what she was doing was the most important thing in the world at that moment. They'd also shared an instant attraction, and like Grant, Ross had given her space, subtly letting his desire for her be known, but letting her come to him when she was ready.

But when she met Ross, she'd been free. She had Katie now, which meant her daughter came first. A casual fling was impossible.

And then she laughed. As if she knew anything about casual flings! She remembered one weekend when she'd taken Katie to Dallas and discovered her sister there on a rare visit home. She'd listened with wonder and disbelief when she inadvertently overheard her mother and sister casually discussing the qualities a woman looked for in a lover.

She'd hardly dated in high school. Except for that never-to-be-sufficiently-regretted hookup with one of Ross's comrades soon after his death, her husband had been her only lover. She'd let Marge talk her into going out that time a year ago, pushed herself to see what it would feel like to let the man kiss her goodbye, and been so embarrassed and uncomfortable afterward she'd never wanted to see the guy again.

It wouldn't be smart to invite an episode like that with a client she was going to have to see repeatedly over the next several weeks while she completed his cabin.

But she couldn't exactly snub him, either. So far, he'd respected the limits she'd set and didn't deserve to be treated with coldness. Besides, he was so warm and engaging, luring her into talking with him, she wasn't sure she could remember to remain distant anyway.

Like Ross, he was a good listener, skilled at drawing people out. Maybe a quality he'd acquired working with injured vets, or the result of the counseling he'd mentioned. However he'd mastered the art, she'd told him much more about her life than she'd ever intended.

Yet she wasn't embarrassed afterward, as she would have expected. Because he'd listened with sympathy, and then responded by revealing something personal about himself. Mentioning griefs he'd lived through, things that had mattered.

They'd shared experiences, like friends do. Despite the pesky attraction she didn't quite know how to handle, she liked him.

Okay, so she'd let herself be his friend. But that was all.

And she'd keep in mind that the friendship would have to become much more distant once the commission was finished. As she repeatedly told Marge, she simply couldn't afford to give up her evening work time to go on a date. Those evenings with the girls were the only breaks she allowed herself.

It wasn't just her own independence she needed to protect, she reminded herself. She couldn't have Katie, who already doted on Grant, get used to having him around permanently, either.

TWO HOURS LATER, the map details squared away and the teacup lamps finished, ready for packaging and mailing, a freshly showered Abby climbed into her truck to drive to Marge's. Enough agonizing and analyzing, she told herself as she put the truck in gear. During this peaceful drive on mostly deserted roads, she would put all thoughts out of her head and simply enjoy the beautiful, golden, burnished-by-the-setting-sun countryside.

Soothed as always by that calming vista, half an hour later she parked in front of her sister-in-law's modest house on the outskirts of the Barrels district in Whiskey River proper. After rapping at the door, she walked into the living room, where three little girls were sitting, their rapt attention on a movie.

Spotting her, Marge got up from the chair beside the couch and came over to give her a hug. "They loved the new movie so much, we had to come home and watch the prequel again."

"Why am I not surprised?" Abby said with a laugh. Walking over, she dropped a kiss on her daughter's head. And received an absent pat on the hand in response.

"I've been replaced by an animated cartoon," Abby said as she followed Marge into the tiny kitchen on the other side of the open-plan room. Donating their sweat equity to a builder Marge knew, she and her sister-in-law had transformed both their small cottages, removing walls to turn the tiny separate rooms into a more spacious area that allowed them to cook or chat in the kitchen while still keeping an eye on children watching TV or doing homework on the table in the adjoining dining area.

"Did you have a good work session?" Marge asked.

"Yes, it was very productive. Got the Texas map cut out and the shiplap backing cut, glued together and clamped. Just have to attach the map once the glue sets. And I finished the rest of the teacup lamps! They're all ready for you to package up and mail when you come out next week. Amazing how much you can get done without 'little interruptions.'"

"Your fingers must be tired and your shoulders must ache. I figure you are ready for this," Marge said, handing Abby a glass of wine.

"You are a goddess," Abby said, taking the glass and downing a satisfying sip.

"So. How was your date with Grant?"

Abby choked, almost spitting out the wine. "It wasn't a date! He wanted to learn how to make a map out of tin roofing. We were working in the shop."

"It was just the two of you," Marge pointed out.

"Right. Just like there's often just two people in a small workshop. It was business, Marge."

"Are you going to see him again?"

"Considering that I haven't even started putting items into the cabin yet, that would be a 'yes,'" Abby said drily.

"That's not what I meant and you know it. Are you going to *see* him? And don't just shake your head 'no' without even considering it. Look, I know the guy last year kind of left a bad taste in your mouth about dating, but there *are* nice guys out there. Ross was one. Seeing a nice guy could ease you into having a life of your own again."

"Right. Are you listening to yourself, Mrs.-I-would-have-shot-him-if-I-coulda-reached-my-purse?"

"Well, yeah, but you didn't have that awful experience!"

Once again, she resisted the opportunity to confess her lapse. But beyond that, the need to remain independent, to not have her happiness tangled up with depending on a man, surged to the fore.

*Ross hadn't been unfaithful, but she'd been abandoned just the same. By the one person she'd loved and trusted, the only person who'd ever valued her. The one she thought put her above all others. Except his bond with his Marine buddies had been stronger.*

She knew her bitterness was unreasonable. He'd been a serving Marine. You go where you're sent. But he hadn't *had* to take that last deployment, her hurt-little-girl heart still answered. He'd volunteered.

Shaking off the memories, she said, "Please don't tell me again Ross would want me to move on."

"I won't, because you already know it. I'm just waiting for you to do something about it. Ross loved you so much, Abby—as he should have! You're a wonderful person. A wonderful person who deserves to have an equally wonderful man to share her life with. Don't deny yourself that forever, please! Out of grief, or some crazy sense that you'd be betraying Ross by finding someone else. You wouldn't be. You know that, too, don't you?"

Did she? Was she holding on to the memory of Ross as the perfect shining knight because of how much she valued him—or only to protect herself from getting hurt again? Using her need to build the business as a shield as well?

She'd told herself she needed to be independent. Maybe she needed to be a little more courageous too.

Maybe Grant McAllister could be the man to inspire her courage.

"Maybe I will do something about it."

"Well, woo-hoo! That calls for more wine. You'll go out

with Grant if he asks you, then?"

"I'd consider it. But probably not anytime soon. You know better than anyone how many orders I have to fill."

"I should confiscate your wine," Marge said, disgruntled. "Just don't wait too long. You can balance work with having a life, you know. Lots of single moms do it."

"Good for them. Give me a little more time, won't you? Right now, I get all the distraction I can handle from Mother."

"Ah, that's why you're in such a sour mood. You're going to Dallas tomorrow, aren't you?"

Abby sighed. "Yes," she admitted.

"Having a friend in Whiskey River to unwind with, talk to, could help offset the aggravation of your trips to Dallas."

"But I already do. I have you."

"Thanks, girlfriend, but you know that isn't what I meant. Good grief, Abby, I'm not saying you have to *marry* the guy. How could it hurt to have a congenial companion, one who's handsome and personable and of the male persuasion? To share a glass of wine with, go to a movie with, go out to dinner with?"

*Ride the ranch with. Skip stones with. Kiss.*

"If Grant says he can be just a friend, you should believe him," Marge was saying.

Yes, but could *she* do only that? Remain only friends with a man who made her starving senses *crave* like a hungry man outside the door of a banquet?

Maybe she should reconsider having that fling? Satisfying her long-denied sensual needs while holding on to her independence.

Like a mistimed handball shot, the memory of that long-ago hookup bounced back to slap her in the gut.

Not a fling, then. Besides, even if she didn't still have that memory to overcome, adding a sexual element was the best way to ruin a budding friendship before it had hardly begun. To say nothing of potentially sabotaging the designer-client relationship.

Not. Possible.

Which brought her back to square one. "Grant is a client, Marge. It wouldn't be professional, and could become downright awkward, to *date* someone you're supposed to be working for."

"I suppose that's true," Marge admitted—and then brightened. "But you won't be working for him forever. By the time you finish the project, you should be great friends. You could start dating him then."

Marge had offered her a straw to exit the conversation, and she grasped it. "Yes, maybe by then."

Would she be ready by then? So many unanswered questions she didn't want to deal with right now. Pushing them away, she said, "Shall we refill our glasses and finish watching the movie with the girls? Disney is more my speed than dating."

"You're hopeless," Marge muttered, but dutifully poured

more wine.

An overnight with her best friend, dinner with the girls, and a movie with her daughter were enough for Abby right now. No matter what her unfulfilled senses were urging.

# Chapter Twelve

THE FOLLOWING AFTERNOON, back at the Triple A Ranch, Grant finished lunch with Duncan and Harrison in the spacious kitchen. "If you boys leave the dishes on the table, I'll get them later," Harrison said as she got up, then dropped a kiss on Duncan's head as she passed him. "See you later, Grant."

Duncan caught his wife's hand and gave it a brief squeeze. "You don't need to bother. Go work on the books. We're perfectly capable of rinsing the dishes and putting them in the dishwasher."

Her eyes tearing up, she gave Duncan a nod and walked out.

"Shall we take our coffee out on the deck?" Duncan suggested as he poured Grant another cup.

"Sure," Grant said. Something was up with Harrison. Given the brief marks of affection the two had shared before she left, it didn't seem to be a problem between husband and wife. Grant wondered if he should ask Duncan about it—he really liked Harrison and was sorry to observe she was upset—or just mind his own business.

Though, when he thought about it, Duncan had seemed a little more distracted than usual during the meal. It was subtle enough that he hadn't paid attention—until he saw the tears on Harrison's face.

Still debating whether or not to say anything, Grant followed his older brother out onto the deck that overlooked the meadows to the west. "Did you finish the sorghum meadow yesterday?" Duncan asked.

"Yes. The Johnson grass on the southernmost meadow should be ready in a day or so, and the Bermuda is about tall enough for another mow."

Though Duncan nodded, his gaze was fixed on the far horizon. Grant wasn't sure his brother had even heard him. His concern deepened—but if something were wrong, surely Duncan would tell him—wouldn't he?

"You getting enough time to work on the cabin?" Duncan asked.

"Not as much as I'd like, but it's coming along. I went out to Abby Rogers's workshop yesterday and put together most of that roofing-tin Texas map I told you about."

"Good."

Grant waited, but his brother added nothing else. Something must be amiss. After tossing out that conversational teaser, he would expect his brother to be all over it, ragging him about how he'd "studied" the technique of cutting tin, maybe standing behind his beautiful blond tutor, his arms wrapped around her, his hands on hers as she handled the snips?

He only wished he'd thought of that method yesterday, Grant thought, distracted—and aroused—by the idea of Abby in his arms. Heck, he'd been in a semi-permanent state of arousal every time he was around her since the day they met, struggling to keep a handle on his desire.

But bottle it up he had to, because, though he was certain she felt the attraction sizzling between them, she'd still not given him the verbal go-ahead he needed to act on it. And he wasn't about to move ahead without that and risk ruining everything before it started.

Besides, having her in his arms while working with razor-sharp tin would have been a very bad idea.

If he was patient enough, he was certain it would happen . . .

And then he realized while he'd veered off—again—into thinking about Abby, his brother had said . . . exactly nothing.

Something was definitely wrong. Might as well forge ahead.

"Okay, so what's up? Harrison is obviously upset and you've hardly heard two words I've said."

Duncan sighed. "Things had been going so well. But that's ranching, isn't it? You think you've brought the bronc under control, then get bucked off on your head."

"Why? What happened?"

"I don't remember if I told you, but we had some trouble

on the Scott half of the ranch last spring. Fences cut, streams dammed up. I'm pretty sure our favorite high-school-bully-turned-real-estate mogul was responsible."

Grant groaned. "Marshall Thomason?"

"The one and only. After Harrison inherited the Scott place from her daddy, Marshall tried to convince her to sell it to him. He thought, as the city girl she was then, she'd not be interested in hanging on to a ranch, especially if it was nothing but trouble. Can't blame him for that, at least—I tried to buy her out for the same reason." His brow lightened for a moment and he chuckled. "Ordered me off the property after I made the offer too."

"Right, but you wanted to buy her out to get back what was originally Triple A land. I'm guessing Pretty Boy wanted to carve the ranch up into condos."

Duncan shook his head in disgust. "Can't you just imagine Thomason's ultra-modern glass-and-chrome condos crowning our old camping ridge?"

"Makes me want to gag. Although chrome and steel would make it a good lightning rod. A place built like that might not last up there very long. But how's that related to what's wrong now?"

"Some of the old guys in town had noticed strangers driving around last spring. I suspect Thomason might have hired them to cause trouble, so I tracked him down. Of course, he denied knowing anything about it. I warned him that if 'accidents' continued to happen, I'd get Brice to come in with tracker dogs and trace who was doing the damage. Things calmed down for a while after that."

"But they've started back up again? Why didn't you tell me?"

"At first, I thought the damage was coincidental. The cows can get feisty, especially after we put the bulls in with them. Two or three times the last two weeks, I found broken fences, but now that we have most of the herd in the western meadows, there's really no place for them to roam. They generally don't like swimming the river, and that forms the boundary beyond the fences along most of our western border. But last night . . . last night, someone cut the fence along the farm road that runs down to 177. I guess the cows heard them, and Mahan—Harrison's daddy's favorite bull— must have gone to investigate what sort of critter was trying to sneak into his harem. He went through the break, down the hill, and got onto the road. There's a blind curve there, you'll remember. Someone came around it and hit him."

"Is he going to be okay? What about the driver? A thousand pounds of bull can do some damage!"

"The driver was shaken up, but no serious injuries. His car was totaled, of course. Mahan wasn't so lucky. The vet said the internal injuries were serious, that he must be in tremendous pain. We had to put him down."

"No wonder Harrison looked so sick! Her daddy's bulls are like pets to her."

"They are a lot more than pets. Mahan was our top-earning herd bull. Harrison has standing orders every year from breeders who want his offspring. Considering that we'd only just put him into pasture with the cows, we're losing probably twenty or more guaranteed sales. Plus now we have to redivide the herd and put more cows in with every bull, which will almost certainly drive down our successful pregnancy rate and result in even fewer offspring. And you know what that means."

Soberly Grant nodded. "Fewer offspring, lesser quality, fewer calves sold and for lower prices. Are you going to ask Brice to look into this?"

"Not much to go on. The wires on the fence last night were definitely cut, but the other breaks could have been cattle pushing through. I'm certainly going to keep a watch on it. If I find anything that remotely looks like it could be pursued, I'll give Brice a call." He shook his head. "Wish it weren't so expensive to string some electric wire along the fences. A break in them would send an immediate alarm, maybe fast enough for us to get out and take a look before any interlopers got away."

"If this keeps up, we might need to go for electrifying at least the border fences."

"We'll see. In view of the sudden deterioration in our financial condition, I'm reluctant to do something that would add to the capital expenses."

"Maybe once I get all the mowing caught up, I could experiment with running wire. I hear the process is pretty straightforward. Then we'd just have the expense of the wire itself—and the electricity, but that shouldn't be much."

"We'd need somewhere to access the current. Which would mean getting a generator at least, or asking the power company to add a pole. Neither of which would be cheap."

"Might be cheaper than losing another herd bull."

"Don't even think that. Harrison would go ninja on me if we lost another of her daddy's bulls." Duncan grinned wryly. "It was bad enough that the bad thing about the good weather this spring and summer was the great hay harvest we're having. But if we have great hay, everyone has great hay, so the price we can get for any surplus will be less, and we'll have to ship it farther away to sell it. And my truck died; I've been using Harrison's. Tony at the repair shop downtown says it's going to need a new transmission— despite how I've babied it on every unpaved trail all these years! Glad as I am to have you back in Whiskey River, I'm beginning to be sorry I convinced you to take the job. I . . . I'm not sure I'm going to be able to pay you the salary I offered."

So that was what was making his brother so uncomfortable. "Okay, that's a blow, but it's not insurmountable. I still have income from my San Antonio job."

"I know, and that makes me feel a little better. But it's part-time, so you're not going to be making what you're used to."

"My living expenses here are pretty low, though."

"True. But you're also in the middle of renovating that cabin. Solar panels? Gas stove insert? A whole set of kitchen appliances and fixtures for a bathroom? None of that comes cheap. I know you've taken out a loan so you can get exactly what you want for it. I'm sorry, Grant."

"Don't worry about it. As long as there's enough to keep the ranch going, we'll make it. We always have. We always will."

"Thanks for being so understanding. But I still feel like . . . I let you down."

"That's my über-responsible big brother talking. You just worry about consoling Harrison and keeping the ranch running. I can take care of the cabin and the salary issues."

"If you can come up with any ideas to generate more cash flow, I'd be happy to hear them."

"Something other than selling the ridge to Thomason?"

Duncan shuddered. "Right. That would be over all three of our dead bodies. Harrison suggested renting out her daddy's house, but I'd hate to have to do that. It wouldn't be as bad as having a condo stuck right in the middle of the ranch, but in addition to evicting you, it would mean having strangers living on our land."

Duncan blew out a breath. "I thought, once we'd gotten the ranch back to its original size, all our problems would be over. I wasn't thinking like a rancher."

"Where the only thing worse than the current disaster is the one waiting up ahead?"

"Exactly."

"That's why you have family, bro. We'll get through this. Let me chew on it for a while. Maybe I can think up some ways to generate more cash. Now I'd better get going. That meadow isn't going to mow itself."

"Right. And if we have any extra hay, sorghum generally sells for more. We're going to need every extra penny we can squeeze."

"Thanks for lunch. And Duncan—don't worry so much. We're a team, remember? And we have Harrison now too. It's not all on your shoulders anymore."

"Thanks, Grant. Shoot, listen to me running on like a nervous greenhorn before his first bronc ride! When I should be asking how you're getting along with that hot babe who's going to furnish your cabin."

So he had been right, Grant thought, suppressing a grin. Duncan hadn't heard a syllable he'd uttered about his visit to Abby's workshop. He wasn't about to enlighten his brother now and invite the next Great Inquisition.

"She may be hot, but she's also a terrific designer. I'm really excited about the décor she's going to create for the cabin."

"If her work is as lovely as the lady, it should be something else." Duncan shook his head. "Small as Whiskey River is, somehow, I'd never met her before."

"Probably because you've never been in the market for new stuff. Everything in this house dates to our childhood.

You ought to take a look at Abby's showroom, let your bride do some redecorating. Hidden Treasures is a small business, which means she has to file a bunch of tax forms. Maybe you could work out a trade, pick up some items in exchange for Harrison doing her tax filing."

"Maybe I should. Getting something new might help console Harrison for losing Mahan. And the scenery at the showroom would certainly be fine. The last time we were in town, Harrison pointed Abby out to me at the grocery story. Woo-hee! If I weren't completely in love with my wife, I might be thinking about hiring a decorator."

"To redo the ranch house?" Grant laughed. "Throw a rope over that runaway thought, bro. Abby's only interested in me as a business client."

"She may say that, but what about you? When you left San Antonio, you left what's-her-name behind, too, didn't you? Ready to move on? If I were examining the field, my eye would certainly linger on Abby Rogers."

"Okay, I'll admit I wouldn't mind moving beyond a business arrangement. Even at that, though, Abby's made it clear that friends is the most she might consider. I'm fine with that. I spent some time on the ranch with her and her daughter, Katie—who's a darling, by the way—when they came up to inspect the cabin. They were both fun and for now, congenial companionship is all I'm looking for."

"Came up to the cabin, did she? Harrison told me the word around town is the pretty widow says she's too busy to date. But if any guy is nice enough to change her mind, you would be, little brother."

"Thanks for the vote of confidence," Grant said drily. "Friends and business associates will do for now. I wouldn't want to try anything more complicated until after she completes the cabin. I'm counting too much on filling it with her designs to risk messing things up before she finishes."

"Well, it's Saturday, whether the cows recognize the weekend or not. The weather is supposed to remain dry, so another day of delay before mowing that meadow won't matter very much. What do you say we watch a baseball game and throw back a few beers? All work and no play, ya know. We'll both feel better."

"You don't have to make that offer twice!"

"Done. Let me toss the dishes in the dishwasher. You grab some beers and turn on the game."

Grant was glad Duncan had shared his concerns about the ranch—something his tight-lipped, do-it-all-myself brother probably wouldn't have admitted before he had agreed to move back and work with him, Grant thought as he took two beers from the fridge. But he was more concerned than he wanted his brother to know about the ranch's unexpected losses.

He'd accumulated a fair amount of savings while he was in the Corps, but he'd plowed the largest part of it into the condo he'd bought in San Antonio and most of the rest into ordering materials and equipment for the cabin. Then he'd taken out the loan Duncan had mentioned to cover the rest. Working at the salary his brother had originally offered along with the rental income from his condo, he could meet all his obligations without any problem. Depending on how much of a cut he had to take, that might no longer be the case.

He could speak to his boss in San Antonio and see if he could pick up a few more hours of salaried work. Although he wasn't sure how he'd be able to take on more clients, keep up with his ranch chores, and still have time to work on the cabin.

But he wasn't about to add to his brother's worries by talking about his own difficulties. He'd do what he promised instead. Consider ways he might be able to increase his own cash flow.

The first, most obvious possibility dampened his spirits enough that he took a swig from one of the beers without waiting for his brother to join him.

He could cut back on the number of items he had Abby create for the cabin.

He didn't want to, but he also wanted to be able to pay her for the work she did. Running a small business, she probably didn't have any more excess cash sitting around than the ranch did.

The idea of letting her down by not purchasing all the items he'd asked for further depressed him. The image of having to go to her, hat in hand, and apologize for being unable to honor their original agreement made him squirm inside.

But he didn't see any way around it. Dialing back on the cabin renovation was the easiest way to cut expenses. He couldn't do without bathroom fixtures and kitchen appliances—though he could investigate buying the least expensive models available—but he could get by with just the bare essentials of chairs, tables, and housewares.

No matter how much he hated the idea.

He could always order more later, when things improved on the ranch. That realization buoyed his spirits a little.

But it didn't make him much happier about the conversation he was going to have to have with Abby when she got back from Dallas.

# Chapter Thirteen

THE FOLLOWING WEDNESDAY, taking a midafternoon water break from cutting the meadow he was working on, Grant got the text message he'd been waiting for and dreading. Abby was back and had some new items for him to look over. He was welcome to stop by any afternoon after he finished work to inspect them.

He could put off the visit, but the mowing had gone well and he expected to finish earlier today than he'd anticipated. The news he needed to deliver wasn't going to get any better if he procrastinated about telling her, so he might as well get it over with sooner rather than later.

Besides, he didn't want her to start finishing the items she'd found specifically for him when he probably couldn't afford to buy many of them. But a reduction in his purchases meant there would be a drop in the income she'd been expecting too. And that grated.

A man took care of a woman, helped her out, protected her. He didn't let her down and make her life more difficult.

He hated knowing he was doing that to Abby. But he hated being dishonest more, so he needed to level with her as soon as possible.

Like today.

With a grimace, he finished off the water. After texting Abby back to say he'd stop by this afternoon, he climbed back up onto the tractor and put it in gear.

SEVERAL HOURS LATER, Grant turned his truck down the drive that led to Hidden Treasures. He'd purposely made sure he arrived while it was still normal business hours, hoping Abby's friend Jillee would still be watching Katie so he wouldn't have to deliver his news in front of her daughter.

It was bad enough to know he would be letting Abby down. Even though her daughter probably wouldn't realize the significance of what his reduced order meant for her mother's income, somehow it made it worse to envision the Princess being present when he made his confession.

So as he pulled the truck up in front of the house, he was relieved to find Katie with Jillee out on the patio. After walking over to greet them and having Jillee confirm that Abby was expecting him, he promised to share a lemonade with Katie after he talked with her mother and continued on to the workshop.

He knocked and waited for the soft tones of Abby's voice telling him to come in. Then he opened the door, saw her, and stopped short.

She wore the chambray work shirt she favored, the sleeves rolled up over heavy work gloves, the shirttails tied at her waist to display her shapely behind in a pair of well-worn jeans. Her blond hair was twisted in a knot and clipped on top of her head, showing him the long, lovely curve of her neck.

As she looked up at him, that aura of innocent beauty that had struck him so forcefully the first time he saw her hit him again, robbing him of breath and setting off an odd little ache in his chest. For a moment, the troubling news he had to deliver went straight out of his head.

Then she smiled and walked over, halting beside him to gaze up. She said something—hello, probably—but he didn't really hear her, mesmerized by the blue of her eyes, the sweet curve of her lush mouth, the smooth skin dusted with freckles and a dirt smudge on her cheek.

He wanted to wipe it off with his thumb. Hell, he wanted to kiss her, pull her into his arms and just hold her loveliness close, treasure knowing that such sweetness and beauty existed in this often difficult and unforgiving world.

Wanted to, but didn't, of course. Instead, he got his frozen jaw working and said, "Did you have a good trip?"

"Very successful. We discovered a new shop on the way back that turned out to be a gold mine. Katie found several old dolls"—she pointed to her daughter's work bench—"that I'm going to help her clean up. We scored three, count 'em, three old farm sinks in good enough condition to refinish, two old hutches, and a bunch of assorted smaller tables. Plus I filled the back of the pickup with old kitchen utensils and three carefully packed boxes of teacups. The owner is holding the rest of the big stuff until I can come back and pick it up. I've made some sketches of what I think I'll do to finish the pieces and have an idea of where I'll place them. Shall I show you?"

Now that she'd given him a perfect opening to deliver his news, he felt compelled to stave off the disappointment he'd be causing her for another minute or two. Plus, he genuinely wanted to know.

"How'd it go with your mother?"

Her smile vanished. "It was . . . more awkward than usual."

"I'm sorry to hear it," he said. As her expression went from calm to troubled, he wished he'd just plowed ahead with his confession and not asked about her trip. Especially when, to his dismay, she looked away, tears sheening her eyes.

He was putting a hand on her chin, tilting her head back up, before he knew what he intended. "What happened?"

It was an indication of the depth of her distress that she didn't immediately push his hand away. Attempting to recapture a smile, she said, "I'm probably making way too much of it. It's just . . . Katie's my whole w-world."

Taking Abby's elbow, he led her to the stools by the workbench and sat her down. "So, tell me."

He thought she might try to draw back, put him off, but somewhat to his surprise, she nodded. "I should have known something was up. We arrived to find this fancy play kitchen set up in Katie's room—toy stove with burners that lit up, fridge with ice dispenser that spit out wooden ice, microwave that went 'ding,' plus all the kitchen equipment and utensils to go with it. Katie was enchanted, of course. Then, in addition to the usual assortment of new clothes, Mother had a rack of fancier-than-party dresses she insisted Katie try on. She loved them too—what little girl doesn't love dress-up? Though Mother was disgruntled when Katie said she'd rather have Snow White and Princess Anna dresses. Throughout the weekend, she kept asking Katie what she wanted, feeding her pizza and candy even though I objected, and every day, there was some new toy or dress. Like each day was Christmas or her birthday."

She sighed. Concerned by her distress, Grant stayed silent, waiting for her to continue.

"Then, when we'd finally stayed long enough that I felt we could leave, Mother casually asked Katie if she wouldn't like to stay at Mimi's—Mother would die if anyone ever called her 'Grandmother'—for a week or two, so Mommy could go back and work undisturbed. Honestly, I could have strangled her! Thankfully, Katie very politely said 'no,' much to Mother's displeasure."

"That's a relief," Grant said, annoyed on Abby's behalf about her mother's underhanded tactics. "I can imagine how unpleasant it made the weekend, but thankfully, problem avoided."

"Avoided for now. But the whole episode makes me really uncomfortable. I can't afford to buy Katie such expensive bribes! Right now, she's still young and would rather be with her mommy. But what about in a year or two or three? When she's less attached to me, and we maybe have more to argue about. What if Mother tries to lure Katie away then?"

Grant gave the arm he still held a squeeze. "Your mother can't whisk your daughter away without your permission. You have guardianship rights."

"I know. Like I said, I'm probably blowing the whole episode way out of proportion. I really can't see Mother wanting to take on the responsibility of tending to a little girl, even for a couple of weeks. It would interfere with her salon appointments and all the lunches and shopping trips with her friends. But just the possibility that she might . . . scared me. I couldn't wait to get Katie away."

"Of course not! I can understand why it rattled you, but just remember, your mother has no authority to take away your princess," he tried to reassure her, furious with her conniving mother—who hadn't bothered to support her daughter growing up, and was still trying to manipulate her.

Tears in her eyes again, she shook head. "I'd be l-lost without Katie."

When her voice broke again, he couldn't restrain himself any longer. Grant pulled her into his arms while she wept on his shoulder.

She let him hold her for a few precious minutes, while he savored the touch of her slim body against his, before she pushed against his chest and he had to let her go. "Sorry, I'm so sorry!" she exclaimed, swiping at her wet eyes. "I promise, I don't usually fall apart in front of clients."

"I hope I'm more than just a client—I hope you consider me a friend. Don't worry yourself to a frazzle over this, please. You'll figure out the right way to handle it. Maybe you should not visit so often—after all, it's not like you have a legal visitation order you have to follow. You're doing your parents a favor by taking their granddaughter to see them. Maybe you should call your mother before your next visit and insist on some limits. Like no more extravagant purchases and no trying to bribe Katie to stay, or you won't bring her to Dallas at all."

Brightening a little, she nodded. "You're right. I've been so upset, I haven't been thinking straight. I don't have to let Mother make the decisions. Katie is my daughter. I'll try to do right by my parents, but if they want to see her, they will have to abide by my rules for her."

"As they should. You're her mother."

"Thanks for listening, Grant. I've been so worried, and I didn't dare talk about it to Marge or Jillee in case Katie might overhear. I guess Mother tried to rule my life for so long, when I'm back in her house, I keep forgetting she doesn't have a right to tell me what to do anymore."

"You're not alone in the fight, either, remember. You have friends and family here to back you up."

"And help me plan strategy, if necessary?"

"Exactly."

Suddenly, as if she'd just realized she'd let him touch her, hold her, she jumped up and backed away, her face coloring. "Well, that was an emotional meltdown you hadn't bargained for! So much for acting like a professional businesswoman. Let me go get those drawings and show you what you came to see."

*I'd rather have you in my arms than look at a thousand designs*, he thought. But, recalling what he needed to tell her, he said, "Can you hold off for a minute? I've been looking forward to seeing your designs. But maybe it's a bad news day, because first I have something I need to tell you."

The instant concern on her face made him feel both gratified and guilty. "What is it?" she asked, coming back to take her seat on the stool. "And how can I help?"

He'd thought by ordering items from her business, he'd be helping her as well as turning his cabin into exactly the space he'd always wanted. She might not be so eager to help *him* after he revealed how he was letting her down.

In a few terse sentences, he told her about the loss of their prize bull and the resulting financial implications for the ranch. "So I'm afraid I'm going to have to cut back on my order. I'm so sorry! I feel awful about reneging on our agreement. I'm not sure yet just how much I'll need to cancel. But I thought I should let you know as soon as possible, so you don't invest in too many pieces just for my cabin."

"I'm so sorry to hear about the bull," she said. "Not the sort of animal I would look on as a pet, but you said your sister-in-law fed him out of her hand. Losing him must have been a personal as well as a financial blow. And you don't need to feel bad about the pieces I've bought. All of them can be completed in different ways, so if I end up not using them for the cabin, I can finish them for the showroom or use them on other projects."

"Right. But you might not have bought as many things now if you hadn't been expecting me to take them all. I just hope I haven't created cash flow problems for your business."

"The pieces are a good investment, whenever I use them," she said, avoiding a direct answer. "Well, why don't we look through the plans, maybe decide what your minimum needs will be?"

A little surprised to be let off so lightly, Grant said, "I sure appreciate you being so reasonable about this."

Abby grinned. "What, did you think I was going to go all girly on you and have a hissy fit over you not buying as much as you'd initially thought? Glad to relieve your mind on that score. Listen, I know better than anyone how things can change in an instant. Why don't I go grab us something to drink, and we'll go through the sketches and the floor plans? Would you like lemonade or something else?"

"Maybe water now. I promised to have a lemonade with the princess later."

"Okay. I'll be right back."

Grant relaxed back on his stool. He hadn't really expected Abby to get angry, but he was still relieved that she was taking it so well. He'd definitely try to throw as much business her way as he could.

And he promised himself that eventually, he'd get every piece they'd originally discussed.

A few minutes later, Abby came back with two glasses of water on a tray. After setting it down, she pulled several folders out of a drawer and brought them to the bench before taking the stool beside his.

"So, some things are essential—bath and kitchen fixtures, your gas fireplace insert, the solar panels. And honestly, I wouldn't skimp on those purchases. Getting top-of-the-line quality that will work efficiently and last a long time is a smarter option than buying the cheapest thing available that might break down after a year. As for furnishings, you could do a single new couch instead of the two matching ones; I could look for some thrift-shop chairs to redo in place of the second sofa. Look for an old farm table instead of ordering the one I showed you, and the same for the dining room chairs and the barstools for the island. If you want to cut the labor expense of having me refinish the used dining chairs and table, I could just clean them up and you could use them as-is for the time being; I could always refinish them later.

And remember the wooden crates I showed you for storage in the bedrooms? I could put together several sets of them to use in place of the custom upper cabinets you were going to order for the kitchen. Instead of tile, we could use more of the roofing tin for the kitchen backsplash. You'll need to order cabinetry for the island, but you could order stock pieces rather than custom and use more of the roofing tin to back it instead of the expensive cut stone. I can look for cabinet and door hardware at secondhand stores too. As for linens and towels and kitchen equipment, I can browse the secondhand shops and look for online closeouts—those always give you great savings."

She paused to sip her water, then began again. For the next hour, she went over all the sketches she'd made, referring to the floor plan on where items would be placed—or replaced. By the time she'd done the complete review, Grant was feeling a lot better about what the cabin was going to look like in the short term—even if he still felt bad about not putting as much cash in her pocket as he'd originally thought.

"It won't be quite as polished as I originally envisioned, but it will be completely livable," she concluded. "And very easy to upgrade with more finished pieces when you have the time and cash to do it."

"Or I might find I like the secondhand stuff so much, I'll just keep it as is."

She smiled. "That's always possible."

"Thanks again for coming up with so many great ideas to make this work."

"It will be fun, actually. I made a virtue out of vice when I was first widowed and scraping by on very little income by substituting something cheaper or homemade for more expensive items. Rather than get depressed about it, I turned it into a game to see how much I could save, and especially to find how many uses I could come up with for old, discarded items. It's amazing what people will throw out. Which eventually led me to establish a business based on the concept."

"You sure seem to have a genius for it," he said, struck again by her ingenuity and inventiveness. And her determination to master hard times rather than bemoan them.

"Thank you. I'll just be glad if the end result doesn't disappoint you."

"I'm sure it won't. You have too fine an eye to install something that looks like it's not well crafted or doesn't belong."

"Do you think there might be more of the old roofing tin at the Triple A somewhere? To do the backsplash in the kitchen—and in the bathroom, too, if you'd like. I'd like to sand off any existing rust and clear-coat it with a poly that will prevent it from rusting again and make it easier to clean. Don't need to install something in an area that will get as water-splashed as the kitchen or bathroom that's going to keep trying to rust on you."

"There's probably more around. I'll check. I'll also see if I can turn up more of those old wooden crates."

"And chicken wire, too, if you have some. Although I can get that at the farm supply store for cheap, if you don't locate any. To make the boxes look more like cabinetry in the kitchen, I can frame some simple doors for them and line them with chicken wire. It gives the visibility of glass without the weight or expense."

"I like that idea."

"If you have the time, and want to, maybe you could help me do the construction and installation of the cabinets, island and backsplash. It will allow me to finish faster and save you on labor costs."

Grant shook his head. "I'd be happy to help, but I don't want to cut down any further on how much you're going to make on this suddenly scaled-back project."

Abby shrugged. "If I spend less time finishing the cabin, I'll have more time to fill other orders. It will balance out."

"Then yes, I'd like to help." He welcomed any chance to spend more time with her—as long as it didn't reduce her bottom line any further.

"Good. Let me check online for stock cabinetry and forward you some links. Choose the ones you like best and I'll get them ordered. By the time they come in, you should have the flooring finished in the new addition and the pine floors redone in the main cabin and be ready to install the kitchen and bath vanities. I'll also get the couch on order. When everything is ready to be delivered, I'll text to set up a time that's convenient for you to help me."

"I can drive over here and transport some of the items out to the cabin too."

"That would be helpful. I'll have the island cabinetry delivered to the site, but it would be more efficient to bring the rest of the things in one trip. While I'm waiting on the cabinets, I'll check the online resale sites and secondhand shops for those living room and dining room chairs and the barstools. I'll also keep an eye out for close-outs on appliances, linens and kitchen equipment. Well, I think we've accomplished what we needed to today. Are you ready for that lemonade?"

"Am I ever! I'm also feeling a lot better about the whole project. Thanks, Abby. For not making me feel so guilty about scaling it back. And for having so many great ideas for making it look wonderful even without all the stuff I'd planned to order."

"Shoot, Grant, with the cabin set in that location, it's going to be beautiful no matter what you put in it."

"Maybe, but your vision will make it even more so."

"I hope it does."

"I know it will." Just as the cabin would look even better with her in it. He'd work on having that happen as often as possible.

He waited for her to close the folders, then walked her out.

"Goodness, it's almost dark!" she exclaimed as they went outside. "Must be later than I thought." Waving at Jillee, who rose from her seat on the patio, where she'd been reading a book to Katie, she said, "Sorry! Time got away from me."

Katie hopped off the settee and ran over to meet them. "I'm awful thirsty, Mr. Grant, but I saved some lemonade for you."

"Thanks, Princess. That's very sweet of you."

"Don't worry about it," Jillee told Abby. "Meghan went over to my mom's today, so I'm not in a rush. Katie and I were having fun reading her books, and I didn't want to interrupt your conference."

"Thanks anyway. See you at Marge's tomorrow night?"

"You got it. Bye, Katie. Bye, Grant."

"Katie, will you bring out some glasses?"

"Right away, Mommy!"

"Are you sure you have time for lemonade?" Grant asked Abby as the girl sprinted off for the house. "It is getting late. I probably ought to be on my way. I don't want to interfere with your dinner and Katie's bedtime."

Abby hesitated, angling her head at him thoughtfully while Grant waited, with regret, for her to dismiss him. "You're right, it is almost suppertime. Why don't you stay for dinner."

For an instant, he was so shocked he wasn't certain he'd heard her correctly. "Stay for dinner?" he repeated.

She took a deep breath, which told him she was a little uncertain about the impulsive invitation. "Sure, why not? It wouldn't be very neighborly to send you home this late to eat all by yourself. Katie would be delighted to have your company."

She couldn't possibly be as delighted as Grant was to receive the unexpected invitation. Rather than leap to accept it, he tried to frame a lower-key response. *Better not scare her off by being too enthusiastic, like you're reading more than a meal into this.*

"Let's see," he said in musing tones. "I could throw a frozen hamburger on the grill and sit at home by myself, watching a baseball game, or share a meal with you and the princess. That's a tough one! Sure, I'd love to stay," he said with a grin. "Thanks for asking."

"Shall we go inside and head off Katie? The sun's going down, which means the bugs will soon be feasting on me faster than a starving man on your frozen hamburger. We can have that lemonade in the kitchen."

Grant followed her into the house, marveling at the transition. He'd arrived here feeling frustrated and all-around bad for not being able to follow through on his order. Instead of venting the disappointment she must feel at the diminishment of her return on the job, she'd instead put her mind to looking for ways to complete the cabin at a lower cost. Rising to the challenge, instead of blaming him and resenting him, or retreating at the unforeseen difficulty. And leaving him now as optimistic about the cabin as he was impressed by Abby's calm and resilience.

What a refreshing change from the women he'd encountered in the past! He'd only ever gotten that kind of support before from his family.

SEVERAL HOURS LATER, Grant lingered on the couch, sipping the wine Abby had opened to go with her excellent homemade spaghetti. And smiling down at Katie, who'd fallen asleep beside him after their tenth round of her favorite board game.

Abby leaned over to ruffle her sleeping daughter's hair. "I should have insisted she go to bed an hour ago, but she was having so much fun. And you have been a terrifically good sport, indulging her with all those games."

"What can I say? I'm a prime board game player."

"Next she'll be asking you to teach her poker. Meghan's daddy has been tutoring her."

"I'm a prime poker player too. But I'd better go and let you take Princess into bed."

"You're probably right."

Grant took his glass into the kitchen, Abby rising to walk with him.

He wished he could take Katie's mother to bed. But it was way too soon for that. He should just be grateful for tonight's invitation, which showed she'd grown comfortable enough around him to see him outside of business hours.

It was a good start.

"I wanted to thank you again for listening about the . . . Dallas situation. Opening up my eyes to my options. I feel much better about it now."

"I'm glad it helped to talk. And thank you. I'm feeling much better about the cabin situation—though I still wish we could proceed on the original plans. But I will enjoy working together on the altered ones."

"You're very welcome. I'll be looking forward to it too."

She halted by the door, smiling up at him, her gentle loveliness wrapping around him again while the faint scent of wine and the rose fragrance she wore filled his head. Before his brain knew what his body intended, he found himself leaning down, kissing her.

She gave a soft gasp and leaned into his kiss, one hand going up to clasp his shoulder. And then, before he hardly had a chance to taste her, she pushed against him and stepped back, her eyes going wide, one hand coming up to cover her lips.

He stepped back, too, cursing himself for the lapse, hoping he hadn't just ruined all the progress he'd made in getting himself invited for dinner.

"Sorry, Abby! I—I shouldn't have kissed you. Though you're so lovely, inside and out, I forgot myself. I need to backpedal, I know. Be—businesslike. And now I'm rambling. Sorry!"

Good grief. How lame could he get? Not that he was the world's most experienced guy, but he'd just blown that encounter like a new bronc rider lasting less than a second on his first horse.

He gritted his teeth, waiting for her reaction. Would she slap his face, throw him out? Or even worse, tell him to find someone else to finish the cabin?

He knew he must be blue in the face from holding his breath when she sighed. "I'm sorry too. I guess the wine made me more relaxed than I should have been. I need to be . . . more on my guard."

"You're not going to let my lapse . . . ruin things, I hope?"

"No. We've committed to doing a job, and we'll do it. I'll look online after I get Katie to bed and forward you links to some cabinet possibilities."

"Okay. I'll be looking for them. Thanks again for dinner. The wine was good and the spaghetti was outstanding."

"You're welcome. Good night, Grant."

She held open the door for him, and once he'd gone through it, quickly closed it behind him.

*Good going, cowboy,* he told himself as he walked to his truck. When you ride a new bronc, you go with him, get a feel for the rhythm of his body as he bucks and adjust yourself to flow with his motion, riding at his pace.

He'd told himself he'd go with the flow with Abby and

wait for a verbal invitation to further closeness—and then he hadn't.

In his defense, his body argued, she was pretty irresistible.

*You'll have to do a better job resisting, then*, his mind answered. *You're just lucky she's giving you another chance.*

And boy, was he grateful.

He'd told Duncan he didn't envision anything more than friends, but the way his breath caught and his heart flip-flopped when he saw her, he was starting to think he needed to rethink that conclusion.

He'd told himself he would follow his attraction to her wherever it led.

That trail was looking more and more like it might lead to something more serious, more permanent, than a casual friendship while she furnished his cabin.

Which would be . . . okay, he decided.

A beautiful, talented woman he ached to kiss, who might turn out to be as dependable as his family, was someone too rare to walk away from.

# Chapter Fourteen

A WEEK LATER, Abby sat in her workroom, staring down at her phone. She'd gotten a fabulous deal on some discontinued cabinetry from the supplier she often used in San Antonio, and after Grant approved the design, had been able to get the items sent out to the cabin immediately. He'd confirmed yesterday that they'd arrived and that he'd finished laying all the floors. It was time to text him and have him come out to inspect and approve the other items so she could start finishing them in the workroom and they could begin to install the kitchen and bath fixtures at the cabin.

*You don't need to figure out what to say and how to treat him to send a text*, she told herself as she typed out the message and hit "send." But she *would* have to figure it out before he met her at the workshop and they started on the installation.

Working at the cabin. Together. Alone.

The thought sent a little shiver of excitement and alarm through her.

She was too honest to kid herself and blame the unexpected kiss they'd shared solely on Grant. Sitting beside him, walking beside him, ever conscious of his masculine presence and the desire nipping at her, she'd hardly telegraphed an "all business, do not approach" message.

Asking him to stay for supper had probably been a mistake. No matter that she'd have felt guilty sending him home hungry to eat alone—again—or that Katie was delighted that he'd stayed.

She'd been delighted too. Too delighted. So delighted that she was now worried.

She'd had far less trouble stepping into his kiss and a lot more trouble stepping away from it than she should have had. Even with her brain well aware that getting close was a bad idea.

It remained a bad idea. Grateful as she'd been for his sensible advice about her mother, she didn't dare let herself depend on anyone else. Her concern about him interfering with her concentration on the business had faded, too, since he'd be helping her with her work rather than trying to lure her away from it. But it would be way too easy to depend on her competent, intelligent, concerned friend, Grant. If she drifted ever closer to him, it would be way too easy to end up in his bed.

None of the good reasons for avoiding sliding down the slippery slope into an affair had changed. The fact that she was having a harder time resisting the voice of reason and shutting down a yearning for his touch that grew stronger at each meeting meant she needed to reinforce her vigilance.

And she probably needed to level with him, as he had with her, admitting her desire for him even as she repeated her determination not to yield to it.

Listening in her head to her tortured reasoning, she groaned. This was going to be one awkward conversation. She just hoped she could set things straight without making a complete muddle of it.

Or kissing him again.

So distracted was she, she jumped when her phone dinged to announce a text message. Those maddening butterflies began doing aerial loops in her stomach when she saw that Grant had confirmed he would drop by this afternoon.

Okay, enough analyzing. Time to get back to work on the buffet she was refinishing for the cabin.

HALF AN HOUR later, she heard the crunch of tires on gravel and her heart did another of those little somersaults. Which was so not good.

*You must think business, business, business.*

She stripped off her gloves and walked out to meet him, waiting while he parked by the showroom and climbed down from his truck.

And smiled at her, setting her heart pounding and making the butterflies do barrel rolls in her belly. Putting her hand on her traitorous stomach, she walked over to greet him.

"Hey, Abby! Where's the rest of my welcoming committee?"

"Jillee took Katie shopping with her. Just groceries, nothing exciting, but I'm betting after they drop them off at her house, they'll pick up Meghan from her mom's, stop by the playground at the park and maybe get some ice cream. So your biggest fan may not be back before we're finished."

"That's disappointing, but I'll look forward to seeing her next time."

"If you'll come back to the shop, I'll show you the pieces I'm working on."

He nodded. An edgy awareness of him walking beside her prickled every nerve as she strolled with him into the workshop. Now to deliver "the speech."

After closing the door behind him, she began, "First, I should—" just as he said, "I really need to—"

Breaking off, they both went silent. "Ladies first," Grant said, gesturing to her with a smile.

"I feel really awkward about how things ended between us last time."

"Let me apologize!" he inserted quickly before she could say anything else. "I didn't intend to scare you or try to take advantage. I guess it's obvious that I not only like you, I'm extremely attracted to you, but you set out guidelines and I went over the line. I'm sorry, and I promise to do a better job of walking that line in the future."

"Thanks for the apology, but it's also pretty obvious I'm just as attracted to you. I know, for most people our age, there'd be an easy answer to a mutual attraction. But I shouldn't have encouraged you. I'm not the no-strings-attached-affair kind of girl, which I found out after one spectacularly bad experience not long after Ross's death. One of his single friends had been especially helpful and sympathetic, and hardly aware of what I was doing, I let him offer 'comfort.' I felt awful afterward, so . . . cheap and spineless. Like I'd disrespected everything Ross and I had shared. Then, last year, Marge tried to set me up, convincing me it would work out better this time."

"But it didn't."

"No. He really was a nice guy, and I . . . I let him kiss me. But I felt just as awkward and embarrassed afterward as I had that previous time. Like touching him was just . . . wrong. It's partly that I know all my time and energy needs to be devoted to Katie and my business, but I guess it's also that I just don't feel comfortable being intimate with another man. Sounds pretty pitiful for a woman to admit, but I'd never had a lover before my husband. I guess I somehow feel that part of me still belongs to him. Even though he's gone. Okay, I freely admit that doesn't make any sense."

"Feelings don't have to make sense. They just are."

That gooey-melting-chocolate feeling softened her heart again. "Thanks. For making that mostly incoherent explanation easier. I just felt that I ought to tell you that, despite the evidence to the contrary I gave you last Wednesday night, if you're looking for a fling, you need to look elsewhere. And I'm sorry, after insisting I wanted our relationship to be all business, for seeming to invite the opposite."

"What if what *I'm* looking for isn't a fling, but a genuine friendship? I like you too. I like working with you, riding with you. You're smart, pretty, and intelligent enough to love this land. If something deeper develops, and we both want it, I'd be okay with that, too, but for now, I've got plenty on my plate myself, with the cabin to finish and my work on the ranch and keeping up with my clients in San Antonio."

He paused, still gazing at her. He'd be busy, too, he said. Not crowding her, demanding attention, taking up her work time. He'd continue as he had been—quiet, calm, letting her determine the pace of what happened between them.

"So if I promise to do better, can we start again?" he continued. "I don't want you to be afraid to be alone with me. I don't ever want you to feel uncomfortable around me. Do you think you can trust me again?"

Yes, this was a man she could trust. To protect her from herself, if necessary.

Slowly she nodded. "Yes, I think I can. I'll try to do better, too, and not give you mixed signals that indicate I'm ready for something I'm not."

"As long as we are honest with each other, I think we'll

be okay."

Honest. No trepidation, no game-playing. Admitting what they felt. Protecting each other from going too far.

"I like honest."

"Good. Strictly friends—cowboy's promise."

A lot of her awkwardness and uncertainty alleviated, Abby felt tension ease out of her like a sigh. She was relieved to be able to continue a project that excited her. Happy to have Grant pledge to be a friend, someone she could consult, but who would not try to overwhelm her or take over control, as her family always had.

Or to tempt her into the affair she knew she wasn't ready for.

"Let's look at what I asked you over to see, then. Over here."

She led him to the storage area at the side of the workroom and pulled off a dust cloth. "These are the two overstuffed chairs I found. Sort of square-backed, square-armed mid-century modern. What do you think?"

Grant gave the pieces an up-and-down inspection. "I like the shape. Not so much a fan of the mustard corduroy covering."

"You're not? What a disappointment!" she teased. "I'll remove all the existing upholstery and padding, of course. Rawhide, tanned in a shade to complement the sofa, would be the best material to recover them in, but you need a special, heavy-duty sewing machine to stitch rawhide, which

I don't have, and it's by far the most expensive material. I thought I'd use denim or twill, both of which are sturdy, resists spills and stains once treated, and are easy to clean. I can get denim in a variety of colors from traditional blue jean to stonewashed to black, and twill in just about any shade."

"I like the idea of denim. Sorta goes with the ranch."

"I'd recommend a medium-blue, traditional wash. It will age like your favorite jeans. Black would echo the window trim, fireplace insert, and sconces, but black fabric has a habit of fading to a nasty purple."

"Medium- to dark-blue sounds good."

"Great. I'll get the material ordered. I already have batting, welt cord, tacking strips and the rest, so I can start on them as soon as the material comes in."

After tossing the dust cloth back over the chairs, she led him around the bench to the buffet she'd been sanding. "I thought this would work in your dining room. It's made of heavy oak, so it will last well, and it's large enough to store all the kitchen and table linens you'll need, plus extra dishes or serving pieces. The space under the shelf at the top is big enough for me to mount the rake heads to hold wineglasses. The finish is pretty well shot—a lot of water damage on the top and some burn marks. Rather than strip it and whitewash it, I'd like to paint it a flat matte black. It will stand on the wall opposite the fireplace, and painted black, the size and shape will echo the size and shape of the fireplace insert, anchoring that side of the room beyond the dining table.

"Which is what I envision this piece becoming," she continued, stepping away from the buffet and moving on to remove the dust covering over a sturdy table with thick, turned legs. "Also in rough shape, but the top, unlike the one on the buffet, is salvageable. I'd do the legs in the same matte black and finish the top in a wood stain that complements the flooring."

Stepping farther along, she pulled the dust cover off a set of eight chairs sitting stacked in twos. "Then, for dining chairs, I found these in that warehouse I told you about. The owner told me they came from a coffee shop that had gone out of business. Sort of a straight Scandinavian design. I'd strip the wood and do a whitewashed finish, then redo the seats with a black vinyl for easy upkeep."

Stepping back, eager to get his reaction, she swept a hand to indicate the whole dining area grouping. "So, what do you think?"

"It looks great—or, it will when you're finished with it. Are . . . are you sure I can afford all this?"

"It came out to a lot less than even I thought it would." She named a figure that made him blink.

"You got all those pieces for *that*? I can't believe it!"

She grinned. "I should be ashamed at how low I bargained down the prices. A little indecisiveness, a lot of 'gosh, I like it, but I just don't have the cash,' and two or three walkaways without buying anything, and the owner practically gave them to me."

Grant laughed. "'She is small, but she is mighty.'"

Laughing as well, Abby gave a little curtsy. "I found some great bargains at the fabric store too. A plain, home-spun-weave cotton that can be backed with a tighter-weave for bedroom curtains."

"Curtains? Why do I need curtains? There's no one for miles around to look into the windows."

"Don't you want to be able to draw curtains at night and darken the room so you can sleep?"

Grant shook his head. "Nothing out there to keep me awake but the moon and stars, and I like seeing them. I've had the ceilings vaulted in the master bedroom, with big windows on the wall that faces north, over the ridge and down to the river. I want sleeping in there to be like sleeping under the stars, without the possibility of getting rained on."

"Sounds wonderful." She could imagine the scene too easily. What would it be like to make love and lay afterward in his arms, gazing up at a wide, star-spangled sky?

She made the mistake of looking over at him—and saw in his eyes the same swell of longing she felt. As if *he* were envisioning lying in that bed, entwined with *her*.

*Don't go there.*

Jerking her gaze away, she struggled to recapture her train of thought. What else had she intended to show him?

Rugs. She'd found some rugs. Clearing her throat, she said, "The last thing I picked up were some carpets at another close-out place. Sort of a southwestern design, mostly neutral colors with some blues and ochre. If you don't like them, I'll keep them for the showroom."

Leaning over, she pulled the two rugs from under the table and rolled them out. "This larger one is for in front of the fireplace. The second, complementary one for under the dining table."

"The pattern is good," he said after studying the two for a minute. "I like the colors."

"Good, I'll add them in. I'm still hunting for appliances, but there will be big sales for the holiday, so I'm not worried about finding some at a good price. I'll keep checking the budget sites for kitchen equipment, dishes, pots and pans, and bedding. When I find some I think are suitable, I'll shoot you a text with a picture. You'll need to get back to me pretty quickly, because the great bargains don't usually last long."

"I don't know that you need to send me pictures. If you find some supergood deals, go ahead and get the stuff. By now, I've seen enough to trust you. If you think I'll like it, I probably will."

"Giving me dangerous latitude, cowboy," Abby warned with a smile.

"Just don't ask Katie's opinion. I don't want to end up with pink-teacup bedside lamps and frilly lace curtains."

"I'll keep that in mind. You said you'd finished with the flooring, didn't you?"

"Yes. I'm still working on the shiplap paneling in the

bedrooms and hallway, but the floors are done."

"Great. Then we can start installing the cabinetry and kitchen storage units whenever your mowing schedule allows. Do you still want to get quartz countertops?"

Grant nodded. "Aside from the top appliances you recommended, that will be my only splurge."

"You'll be happy you did it. They wear like iron and have almost zero maintenance. Once we get the base cabinets installed, I'll take some measurements. I know a guy at a big stone yard in San Antonio. He should have some partial slabs and remnants we can use that will be half the cost of buying a regular slab. Plain white or concrete gray are generally the cheapest patterns anyway, which, with the whitewashed wood, Hill Country stone and black accents, I'd envision for the cabin. I'm still looking for the right piece to make into the bathroom vanity, but the farmhouse sink is at the refinishers now and will be ready for when I find it."

Grant shook his head wonderingly. "It's amazing to think of it all coming together."

"The interior work tends to go more slowly—finishing the electrical and A/C and getting the plumbing hooked up. But yes—another few weeks, and you should be able to move in. Now, do you think you could spare an entire day off from mowing? Once we start installing things, it would be more efficient to just keep going."

Grant paused, considering. "Probably. I should have everything caught up by next Tuesday."

Abby clicked through to the calendar on her phone. "I don't have anything scheduled then, so that would work."

"Long-range forecast I saw this morning says the weather's supposed to be good. Why don't you bring Katie? After work, we could take her for a ride around the ranch. One of Duncan's friends has a pony I could borrow for her."

"Katie, having a pony to ride around the ranch with you? She'll think she's died and gone to heaven."

Grant chuckled. "We'll make a good Texas cowgirl out of her yet."

"She will love it! Thanks, Grant. I'm taking another road trip tomorrow, hoping to find the right cabinet to make the bathroom vanity. If I do, we can bring that out Tuesday."

"Good. I'll text you to confirm the time, but I'll plan on meeting you here Tuesday morning, bright and early, to load up all the material and head out to the cabin."

"Okay. I'll pack us a lunch and snacks, so we don't have to lose time heading into town to eat."

"Which will leave us more riding time at the end of the day, the better to reward Katie for being patient while we work."

"She will be so excited! I don't dare tell her about it, or she'll be asking every day whether it's time yet. Well, I'd better get back to work. I'd like to get the rest of that buffet sanded down before Katie gets back for dinner."

"Go ahead and get back to it. I can see myself out."

"Thanks, Grant. For your enthusiasm. And your understanding."

He smiled, holding her gaze, while butterflies soared and chocolate melted and she mixed every goofy metaphor her brain came up with. Then he tapped the tip of her nose with his fingertip and said, "Take care of yourself. I'll see you Tuesday."

"You too. Bye, Grant."

"See you, Abby."

She made herself walk back to the sideboard and pick up the sanding block—although her entire attention focused on listening to his footsteps, the sound of the truck engine firing up, and the pop and crackle of tires on gravel as he drove away.

When the last of the distant sounds faded to silence, a sinking feeling made her sigh. How crazy was that? For her to feel so deflated because he'd just left her.

She'd see him again in less than a week. Before that, she had a ton of work to do here, more items to find, to say nothing of another group of teacup lamps and wall sconces to complete to keep up with her online orders.

Her life was full and satisfying, just as it had been before he walked into her showroom that day over a month ago.

It was silly to feel somehow something would be lacking because she'd not have him in it for a week.

# Chapter Fifteen

I N THE LATE afternoon two days later, Grant stood at the paddock on the Bar T Ranch owned by Mitch Forrester, a friend of Duncan's, watching the Connemara pony he wanted to borrow for Katie. He smiled, envisioning the squeal of excitement when the little girl set eyes on this handsome little mare with her gray-dappled skin and dark-gray mane.

"Pretty little lady, isn't she?" Mitch said.

"A beauty. She'd be perfect."

"Great temperament for a beginning rider. Gentle and easygoing."

"Katie's mother is going to hate me. After riding Moondust, she's going to want a pony of her own."

"She's welcome to borrow this one anytime. I bought her for my daughter when she started to ride. Molly enjoyed riding her, even showed her, but shc's riding competitive dressage on a full-sized mount now. But Moondust is such a sweet little lady, I couldn't part with her. My other horses like her company as much as I do."

"I'm sure my sweet little lady will too."

After arranging to bring a trailer over the following Monday to pick up the pony, Grant was walking back to his truck, when a voice recalled him.

"Grant McAllister! As I live and breathe."

He pivoted at the sound of that vaguely familiar voice. "Linda Randall?"

A rangy brunette in jeans, T-shirt and a cowboy hat walked over. "It's Linda Forsythe now. It's been a few years, Grant! I'm flattered you remember me."

"Of course I remember you. You were the best barrel racer on our high school rodeo team. How are you?" he asked, exchanging a hug with her.

"Doing well. I came back to Whiskey River after my divorce. I'm helping my daddy run the ranch now. I've got two boys, both hot for rodeo and driving me crazy. How are you?"

"Great. I'm back in town helping Duncan run the Triple A, now that it's back to its original size."

"Yes, I heard he'd married Harrison Scott and reunited both parcels of land. I'm glad for him. Getting back that land was all he'd wanted since anyone here could remember, and he's worked damned hard to make it happen. Have you done any rodeo lately?"

"No, not since I left for the Marines. I still enjoy riding, but I've lost the yen to rattle my brain on the back of a horse not happy about my presence. You still whipping around barrels?"

"I do some. Not competitively anymore, though. Would you like to get back into rodeo? It's hard to resist trying to conquer those broncs, once you've got a taste for mastering them."

"I wouldn't mind the challenge," he admitted. "But I'm not sixteen and in school anymore. Thankfully for the well-being of my bones and brain, gainfully employed in running a ranch, I don't really have the time."

"Are you sure? I'm one of the advisors for the high school rodeo team now. The Bar T stables our horses and lets us use their paddock for practice, which is why I stopped by today. I would sure appreciate having you come on board to help out when the kids get back to school next fall. They'd be beyond excited to have a former state champion saddle bronc rider as an advisor. I wouldn't mind . . . consulting more closely myself."

Grant picked up immediately on the subtle change from friendliness to . . . something with a definite sensual under-current. Linda had liked him in high school, he knew. He'd liked her, admired her technique and dedication. She'd been a really good barrel racer—and a very attractive girl, with her long, brown hair, big, dark eyes, and tall, athletic body. If he hadn't been tied up with Sally at the time, he might have followed up on their mutual attraction.

She'd told him she was divorced. The innuendo in her voice, her body language—face angled up to his, her taking a step closer into his personal space—indicated she was interested and available.

It would be easy and convenient to respond. She hinted at just the sort of relationship he'd thought to look for when he moved to Whiskey River, if he began one at all. A classic "no strings attached" casual affair with a companionable woman he admired.

So why did he feel no inclination whatsoever to take her up on the unstated offer, despite the history of attraction between them?

Probably because of a certain lovely blonde who didn't do "no strings attached" affairs.

But he didn't want to turn Linda down so abruptly, she'd start wondering if he'd hooked up with someone else. He'd need to finesse this.

"As I said, I'd love to help out, but I just don't think I'll have the time. Surely not this summer, with all the mowing in full swing. In addition to which, I'm remodeling my grandfather's old cabin with the hope of moving in by the end of the summer. Then comes fall—and you know all the chores that have to be done on a cattle ranch in fall."

"Do I ever!" she said with a rueful laugh. "I've been trying to train my boys to take over some of them. Well, don't dismiss the idea out of hand. Why don't you take another look at your schedule in the fall, once you see how the chores shake out? I'd love to have you join the team at the high school."

Grant nodded. "Fair enough. I'll do that."

"If it doesn't work for you to help out with rodeo, we could always go for a drink some night after you put the cows to bed. Even cowboys need some . . . relaxation. It would be fun to share a beer and talk about old times. Maybe make some new ones?"

She could hardly be more direct than that without offering to go for it here and now on the barn floor. *Right offer, wrong lady*, he thought, suppressing the wry chuckle that might make her think he was actually considering her suggestion.

Once again, he wanted to turn her down flat, but once again, that would invite a speculation he needed to avoid.

So he made himself smile. "An offer like that from such a pretty lady is awful hard to refuse. I'll sure keep it in mind. I don't mean to be rude now, but there's that mowing waiting. Got a meadow to finish up before dark."

"Understood," she said, her tone noticeably cooler, her gaze on him speculative. But fortunately, she decided not to question him further, sparing him the need to dodge any questions about who he might be seeing. "Great to see you again, Grant. I hope later, when you are less *busy*, we can come to a . . . mutually agreeable arrangement."

"Good to see you, too, Linda." After tipping his hat goodbye, he walked to his truck—conscious of her gaze following him until he'd started up the engine and driven off.

He'd received similar come-ons before and had responded to several, though as a rule, he wasn't much for one-night stands. Most of his lovers had been more-or-less longer term. He'd found out early on that he preferred to be intimate with a woman whom he liked to spend time with in *and* out of bed.

All those previous relationships had eventually withered, as the lady grew impatient for a commitment he wasn't prepared to offer, or they both lost interest and moved on. Or, in Kelsey's case, after he'd committed heart and soul, and she hadn't had the grit to last over the long, difficult haul of his recovery.

But if every instinct had him stepping carefully away from Linda's offer without regret, he might already have fallen harder for Abby than he'd thought.

The possibility didn't alarm him much at all.

Maybe he was finally ready to trust a woman again. And since he would have to take things slowly with Abby anyway, he'd have plenty of time to decide whether taking the next step was right for them both.

IN THE AFTERNOON the following Tuesday, Grant paused to survey the cabin. A glow of satisfaction and excitement warming him at seeing it taking shape, he looked over at Abby, who was screwing a door onto the last of the wooden-box upper cabinets they'd mounted.

"Ready to take a water break? We can join Katie on the deck."

"Might be time for her snack too," Abby agreed, finishing the fixture and placing the screwdriver back in her tool belt.

"If the snack is as good as lunch was, I'm going to have to work harder to keep my slim figure."

She chuckled. "Lugging roofing tin, cartons of flooring, hauling cast-iron sinks, oak buffets and other assorted furniture? You probably get enough workout time."

"Does that mean you admire my slim figure?" he teased.

"It's not bad for a man of your age," she shot back. "Stop fishing for compliments, cowboy."

Grant shook his head mournfully. "I don't know. I might need to sit out the rest of the day and rest my ancient bones."

"We have accomplished a lot," she said, gesturing around the room. "The lower kitchen cabinets set, the wooden-box uppers in place, all the doors attached. Island cabinetry in place, just needing us to attach the tin you cut for the backing. Old buffet cabinet set in the bathroom and both sinks mounted."

Grant groaned. "My back may never recover."

"They made those old porcelain-enameled iron sinks to last. But you should feel lucky. A refinished one can sell for upward of five hundred dollars, and we scored both of them for less than a quarter of that."

"Stealing candy from babes, like you did to get the dining furniture? Don't you feel guilty?"

"Not a bit. The owner of that secondhand shop has crews that demolish old houses in the areas being redeveloped as Houston, Austin, San Antonio and Dallas spread out to eat up the surrounding countryside. It results in him acquiring a large inventory that he prefers to turn over quickly rather than keep and invest the time and money to get the salvaged pieces restored. If I did get a steal of a deal, put it down to being outraged on behalf of all those character-filled old houses being pulled down to make room for endless developments of cookie-cutter places sold to flash young professionals working in the city who never use the kitchen anyway because they dine out or live on takeout."

"That's quite an indictment," he said, amused by her passion in defense of old houses.

"Can you tell that Mother—who can hardly boil water— insisted on putting in a farm sink when she had her kitchen remodeled? Not like the ones I bought, though. She looked at some refinished ones her designer recommended, but nothing *used* would do for Mother. She ended up getting a high-end, fired-clay model imported directly from the Swiss manufacturer. Anyway, after our break, we can take the tin you've already cut and put the backsplash up in the bathroom and tack the backing onto the island, and I think we'll be done for the day."

She waved a hand around to encompass the whole cabin.

"Is it beginning to look like the vision you had for it?"

*No, the vision was far better—with her in it.*

"It's going to look just as fine as I'd hoped. I can't thank you enough."

She chuckled. "You are paying me, remember? If you love it, that's all the thanks I hope for."

He could think of some others—like luring her into more of her sweet kisses. Maybe . . . surely . . . soon.

"Katie's been a big help too. I'm impressed with how well she works at the tasks you give her and entertains herself when you don't need her to do something for you."

Abby sighed. "The poor girl has had lots of practice. You've been great about finding jobs for her to do—she really does like to help. And fortunately, she's very imaginative, so she's happy to make up games with her dolls and action figures, or to read her books. It's also fun for her to have the two of us to offer her some attention."

Her darling of a daughter was as beguiling as she was. "Let's go join her. I'm eager to see what's in that snack bag."

They walked out of the cabin onto the front porch, to find the little girl busy with her crayons.

"Hello, Princess," Grant said. "Whatcha working on?"

She looked up at them and smiled. "I made a picture for you!" She handed it over, beaming at him.

"It's a drawing of my cabin!" A five-year-old's rendition of the cabin front, drawn from the perspective of the big rock about twenty feet away, but quite recognizable, with the gray-tan stone walls, the wooden awning over the deck, even the Adirondack chairs on the porch—with three people sitting in them.

"See?" she said, pointing at the stick figures. "That's me and you and Mommy. I'm loving being at your cabin!"

Katie and Abby and Grant—in his cabin. He loved the idea too.

"I'm happy that you love it. I'll treasure this drawing of it. Maybe I can get your mommy to frame it for me. And you know what? You've been such a supergood helper today, after Mommy and I finish our work, we have a special treat for you."

Katie's eyes went wide. "Ooh, we're going fishing?"

Grant laughed. "Not fishing this time, but something just as good. Maybe something even better."

"Thank you, Mommy, Mr. Grant. I'll get ready right now!" She started scrambling to put away her crayons and books.

"Drink your water and have some peanut butter crackers first," Abby said. "It's going to take us a little bit longer to finish up, but we'll be ready soon."

Grinning, Grant tossed back his own water. He was almost as excited to give Katie her treat as she was to receive it.

AN HOUR LATER, after putting away all their tools and

locking up the cabin, they loaded up in their respective trucks and drove over to the Scott house barn. After pulling up by the paddock, the little girl practically tumbled out of her car seat.

Grant jumped down from his truck and loped over to meet her at the paddock rail. "How would you like to go for a horseback ride? On a pretty little pony who's just the right size for you?" He pointed to the Connemara, who was grazing ten feet away.

The expression of awe and wonder on the little girl's face was everything he could have wished for, making him so glad he'd decided to do this.

"I get to ride—her?" Katie whispered.

He looked over her head at Abby, who'd approached behind them and was smiling down at her daughter with tender affection. A gesture that made Grant yearn to have her look at *him* like that.

Turning his attention back to Katie, he said, "You sure can. Her name is 'Moondust.' We're going to get the saddle and bridle from the barn and I'll show you how we put them on. Then we'll get my horse and Mommy's and go for a ride around the ranch."

Skipping and jumping, shouting, "I'm coming, Moondust! I'm coming!" Katie headed for the barn door. Abby followed with Grant.

"I'm going to hate you after this, probably," Abby murmured. "Katie's going to want to move into the barn and live with Moondust. I know"—she held up a hand to stop him from speaking—"we gotta make a good Texas cowgirl of her."

"It is best to start early," he replied, and laughed when Abby groaned.

Katie was as avid a pupil as a riding instructor could ever want. Grant had her climb the paddock fence so she could help him with the placement of the bridle, though her reach wasn't far enough to actually fit it over the mare's head and she wasn't tall enough to help with the saddle. He let her feed the mare apple slices while he tacked up his gelding and Abby's mare.

After he'd helped Katie into her saddle and they'd both mounted, Grant took the pony's reins. "I'll lead Moondust while you get used to being in the saddle. Would you like to go see some cows?"

"Please, no bulls for her to feed out of her hand," Abby murmured to him.

"Don't worry," he murmured back. "Only Harrison's crazy enough to do that."

As they rode along, Katie giggling with glee and exclaiming over the rocks, the trail, the pasture, and the fences, Abby gave a dry chuckle. "I want to hate you for this, I but can't. Katie is enjoying it too much. Thank you for arranging it."

"As the son, grandson, great-grandson and great-great-grandson of ranchers, it's my patriotic duty to make a Texas cowgirl of her. I'm glad she's enjoying it. And that you're enjoying her enjoying it."

"Alright, I admit it, I'm enjoying the ride on its own merits. And the company," she added, looking over at him with a sweet, gentle smile that struck him like a cupid's arrow to the heart.

A feeling rushed through him, like he was in an elevator that had taken a sudden drop. A swooping sense of falling that left him a little dizzy. A little dazed, as he touched a hand to the odd feeling in his chest.

*I'm loving having both of you here, enjoying my world. Enriching it.*

But that was too fervent an avowal, and he didn't want to scare her. So instead, he said, "I'm glad to hear it. Maybe she'll convince you to get a pony after all."

"I wouldn't go that far!" she flashed back, making him laugh.

After ten minutes of easy riding, they reached the first occupied pasture. While Grant pointed out the cows and the bull in the distance, Katie peppered him with questions.

Did all the cows have names? ("No, most have numbers on their ear tags.") Did the tags hurt? ("Ask your Mommy; it's like a lady wearing pierced earrings.") Do they like eating grass? ("They love it.") Is the bull mean? ("No, but he's big and unpredictable, so we won't go into the pasture.")

When Katie expressed her disappointment at not being able to pet the cows, Grant pulled out his next round of tricks. "We can't pet the cows. But I can show you some things with this rope."

He reached for the looped lariat he'd hung on his saddle. "Some ranches still rope and drag their calves when they need to tag and brand them. The Triple A doesn't anymore—unless one tries to escape and we have to—but my brothers and I all learned growing up how to rope."

"Are you going to rope a cow for me?"

"No, I don't want to disturb them. They're busy having fun with their friends. But I can rope something else for you—a tree, a big rock, a fencepost. What would you like?"

Katie pointed to a small cypress growing beside the trail. "Rope that."

"Sure, little lady."

Grant fit the rope to his hand, slid some through the eye to create a loop, raised it overhead and began a slow twirl.

"You don't use your whole arm to spin it?" Abby asked.

"Don't need to. It's all in the wrist. Everything pivots around that, like a wheel around an axle. Then you open the loop wider"—he demonstrated, letting more rope slide through the eye—"twirl it to the right height and . . . release."

Grant swung his arm and cast the rope, which sailed elegantly through the air to land neatly over the cypress tree. Jerking the loop shut, he rode over and offered the rope to Katie.

"Just got yourself a tree, ma'am."

Giggling, she tugged on the rope, making the little tree

bend toward her. "Do it again!"

Chuckling himself, he rode over and retrieved the rope. "What now?"

For the next ten minutes, Katie had him rope everything in sight—fence posts, two large rocks, several increasingly large cypress trees, and last of all—"Rope Mommy."

Grant swung his gaze to Abby, who shrugged. "Whatever."

"This is going to be fun," he murmured to her, grinning.

His gaze locked on hers, he prepared the rope, twirled and cast it. Let it settle around her shoulders, pulled it snug and gradually tightened his grip, pulling her toward him.

Being a well-trained cow pony used to closing in on roped cattle, Abby's mare obligingly stepped toward Grant's gelding as he reeled in the rope and drew Abby ever closer, until the flanks of the two horses touched.

"Gotcha," he murmured. *Wish I did. Could I have?*

She continued to gaze up at him, surprise, longing—and desire in her eyes?

All emotions he felt even more deeply.

The spell was broken by Katie's delighted laugh. "He caught you, Mommy! You're so good, Mr. Grant! Can you teach me?"

Jerked back to reality, Grant loosened the lasso, pulled it off over Abby's head and let the horses move apart. He realized his heartbeat was thundering and his breathing ragged. After steadying it, he said, "When you're older,

Princess. Your hands are a little too small yet to handle the rope."

"Can you do other tricks?"

*None as fine as capturing your mother. Might want to do that—for keeps.*

"Let me see. Maybe I can." Sliding down from the saddle, he prepped the rope, spun it out into a wide loop, lowered it toward the ground, then jumped through the loop from one side to the other, back and forth. "That's the 'Texas Skip,'" he told her.

Katie clapped her hands. "Do another trick!"

"Okay, but just one more." Beginning again, he spun the rope out to form a small loop, then passed it, flipping from top to bottom, back and forth from one side of his body to the other. "That's a butterfly."

Abby lifted her eyebrows. "I'm impressed. I knew you grew up on a ranch, but I didn't imagine you knew such fancy tricks."

"My brothers and I learned to rope from necessity. Learning tricks was more a brotherly one-upmanship to see who could do the fanciest things with the rope."

Turning back to Katie, he walked over to take up Moondust's lead rein. "We better ride back to the paddock now, Princess. Your bottom will get sore if you spend too much time in the saddle on your first ride."

Katie's smile faded. "Do we have to?"

"It's getting late, Katie," Abby said. "Mr. Grant still has

chores to do with his cows today, and we don't want to keep him too late."

"I could help him," she coaxed.

"You'd be a willing helper," Grant said. "But the cows are still a little too big for you to handle right now. You can help me take the bridles off and put them back in the barn when we get back. Then I have another surprise—if you and your mommy have time for it."

While Abby looked over to him in surprise, Katie said, "I love your surprises! Say 'yes,' Mommy!"

"Let's get the horses back to the barn first, and then she can decide." Keeping hold of Moondust's lead, he walked back to his own horse and mounted.

"I don't love surprises," Abby said with some asperity as they headed back.

"I imagine not, considering some of the ones life has thrown at you." Lowering his voice so Katie, who was singing a song to Moondust, wouldn't overhear, he murmured, "I have some steaks in the fridge back at the house. You were nice enough to cook me dinner last week, so I thought I'd return the favor. If it's okay with you, we'll take them back to the cabin to grill. But I won't mention it to Katie, if you'd rather not do that."

"Since you know she'd be all about it."

"It sure is fun to give her things you know she'll enjoy."

Her smile turned melancholy. "She's so sunny and bright-spirited, hardly ever in a bad mood. Such a willing helper and possesses unusual empathy for a child. I want to give her *everything*."

"Must be hard not to spoil her."

"It is. I do try."

"You've done a great job so far. I don't think I've ever met such a well-behaved, helpful, easy-tempered little girl."

"I imagine your experience with children isn't vast, but thank you. You wanted a price reduction on the project, you said? Nothing melts a mother's heart faster than praise of her child."

*How he'd like to melt her heart.*

"All well-deserved praise—for you both. No price reductions necessary."

They rode back to the barn in companionable silence, listening to Katie as she regaled her pony with her entire repertoire of favorite songs. Grant had always loved riding, especially riding like this, not burdened by chores, just enjoying the beauty of the land to which he belonged, heart and bone.

To be honest, he'd always preferred riding it alone, lost in his own thoughts, with no one's chattering to disturb him.

But it felt so easy and natural to have Abby riding beside him. She seemed as content as he was to simply live in the moment, feeling blessed by the beauty all around him.

The beauty beside him.

He really liked Abby Rogers, and admired her even more than he liked her. He felt compelled to help her and her business.

He hadn't intended for his emotions to get so tangled up in the bargain. The searing episode with Kelsey had left him with a deep reluctance to risk his heart to someone who might not be able to handle the inevitable crises that came to everyone over life's long haul.

But increasingly, he was coming to believe that this woman could.

Would she want to?

He felt an unexpected niggle of jealously at the depth of loyalty her late husband had inspired. Five years, and she didn't seem to have moved beyond his loss. But as Grant knew all too well, grief made its own rules, and they were different for everyone. You couldn't force the process, or decide it was over as a matter of will.

It was entirely a matter of the heart.

As she'd admitted, there was a lingering resentment of the Marine Corps for the brotherhood of commitment that had taken her husband from her—which meant his background in the Corps wasn't exactly in his favor.

But by now, he was pretty sure he was ready to take that chance with his heart again—for her. Believing what they shared would deepen, as he instinctively felt it could, into a lasting commitment for them both.

It would take time—more for her than for him, probably. But he was a patient man. To claim the joy that might be theirs, he was prepared to wait for her to be ready too. Ready to finally give *her* heart again—to him.

# Chapter Sixteen

SEVERAL HOURS LATER, he and Abby sat on the porch, burning citronella candles to shoo away bugs as they watched the last traces of pink, amber, and gold fade in the western sky.

"Gorgeous sunset," Abby murmured.

"Sorry Katie missed it," Grant said, pointing at her daughter, who was sprawled, dozing, in her chair beside theirs.

Abby chuckled. "She had a long day. Carrying in supplies at the cabin, going on her first trail ride, helping you grill steaks. She loved all of it! Thanks for thinking of so many ways to include her in what could have been just a boring work day she'd been dragged along on."

"She's fun to be around. And she is helpful."

"I hope you're pleased with the progress on the cabin. Plumbing in and working, wiring done, and we're getting down to the final finishing. I've taken measurements for the kitchen and island countertops. I'll call my stone guy tomorrow, probably run into San Antonio to pick through what he pulls out for me. Would you like to come along and see it?

Although stealing this whole day, I know I've probably already put you behind on your mowing."

"I'd love to go with you—but realistically, I can't," Grant said regretfully. "I need to be at the ranch every day for the next week or so. Not just for cutting the meadows. There's a new project Duncan asked my help on, measuring some of our property lines to estimate the cost of electrifying it. He's afraid someone may be tampering with our fence lines."

"That sounds serious," Abby said—and then her eyes widened. "Is that how Harrison's bull got into the road? That's awful!"

"We don't know for sure. But we need to watch the lines more closely. Damaging fences is an unforgiveable sin to a rancher, a truth every farm kid learns growing up. You spend enough time repairing the ones the cows break through. I promised Duncan I'd get those measurements done this week. Since he hardly ever asks for help, on the few occasions he does, I never turn him down."

"Of course not."

Grant blew out a sigh. "I wish I could help him come up with ways to eke more income out of the ranch. Harrison offered to rent out her father's house, but neither Duncan nor I really want to do that. To see strangers living full-time in a house on our land."

"I can understand why you wouldn't like that idea. But maybe there's another way to use it. Repurpose it, once you move to the cabin."

"Repurpose it?" he repeated. "How?"

"The simplest way to avoid the privacy issues and problems a long-term renter can cause would be to set the house up as a short-term vacation rental."

"I'm not sure my brother would find that option less objectionable. There would still be strangers tromping around on Triple A land."

Sitting up straighter, her eyes suddenly brightening with enthusiasm, she said, "Wouldn't that depend on the strangers? Because I've just had maybe an even better idea! You have contacts in San Antonio, don't you? Think about how much Katie loved riding her pony and visiting the cows. What about setting up summer day camps for kids from San Antonio—organized through the Y or church programs? You could take kids on trail rides, teach them roping. Maybe let the older ones help with some of the chores in the barn or with the cattle. Teach other kids to learn to love the land, like you are with Katie."

He'd resisted the idea of strangers tromping over the Triple A—but kids? "That just might work!" he agreed, catching her enthusiasm. "Besides the Ys or church programs, there are a lot of military bases in San Antonio. I bet the MWRs would love to set up 'Day Out at the Ranch' programs for the kids in base childcare and summer school. I know I would have loved showing my buddy, Tommy's, kids around."

"Exactly! Your barn's pretty large already, but if you work with the military kids, you might be able to get a grant to expand it, add some restrooms, maybe even a bunkhouse, so you could do overnight or weekend events."

"I'd have to figure out a way to supervise all that and still keep up with the chores, though," he said, his enthusiasm dimming a bit.

"You could double up. If you're bringing in enough income, you could hire some help to do the simpler chores—fixing fences, delivering feed—while you run the program. I understand you McAllisters not wanting outsiders on your land. But how wonderful it would be to share its beauty with city kids who've never experienced anything like it! Visits that might inspire them to love the open country and appreciate caring for livestock like your family does."

"That's exactly why I'd want to do it—if I can figure out the logistics."

Fully engaged now, she rushed on, "There'd be other possibilities, once you got the facility set up properly. You could advertise the barn as a conference center for ag organizations from the universities or county extension services, even cattlemen's associations. You could partner with the B&Bs in Whiskey River to provide housing and some of the restaurants for meals. I bet Hell's Half Acre and the folks at the Diner, Lucy's Pizza, Booze's or even the steakhouse would love to participate. Maybe your brother would consider that too."

"He might," Grant said, his mind whirling at the possibilities. He shook his head wonderingly. "You really are Queen of Repurposing."

Abby gave a delighted laugh. "Repurpose—that's my middle name. Besides, it's so beautiful in the Hill Country! It didn't take me long to come to love it. If it were my property, being here is a blessing I'd want to share with kids who would never experience it otherwise."

"Duncan might go for that idea—not strangers intruding on us, but sharing the heritage we're privileged to be caretakers of with children."

"You'll want to do something with the Scott ranch house when you move to the cabin anyway, won't you? It wouldn't be good for it to just sit empty."

Another thought occurred, which excited him even more. "Since I'll be keeping the horses stabled in the barn there, I could look at setting up a riding program for injured or disabled vets. The VA is always looking for new activities for its members. Just spending time at a place like this"—he swept his hand to indicate the sweeping vista of mountain, valley, and creek—"surrounded by such peace and serenity can help you heal."

She smiled. "It sure helped me."

"I could talk with my boss, too, about using the barn to hold job fairs for our clients, maybe host clients up here for a weekend. There's one in particular, an Army vet who is figuring out how to run again on lower-leg prosthetic devices, who might really enjoy getting up on horseback. He just texted me that he's accepted the job I set up for him as a personal trainer. When you're learning how to live in a body that doesn't work like it used to anymore, it can be a huge morale boost to master a new physical skill. I think it would give him more confidence as he tackles that job."

"Must be satisfying work. You match employment to vets, right? Are all of them injured?"

He was about to launch into a further description of the work he did and how rewarding it was when he remembered her circumstances. "You probably shouldn't get me talking about it. I'm apt to run on, and I know your feelings toward the Corps aren't exactly friendly."

She sighed. "I don't have anything against the people. Quite the contrary! I admire them—you—for your dedication and willingness to do a hard, dangerous job to keep the rest of us safe."

The explanation had been simmering in his mind for a long time. He'd hesitated to voice it, not wanting to anger or alienate her—but maybe it would help. Besides, his work— the Corps—was part of him, part of what had made him into the man he was. If they were to have a future together, she'd need to accept that part too.

Deciding to take the risk, he said, "I know you felt . . . abandoned by your husband choosing to accept another deployment. You can't imagine how much we miss the ones we love when we're gone, how often we dream of them and long to be back home with them. I can promise you, there was nothing your husband wanted more than to come home to his wife and daughter. Doing his job didn't mean he didn't love you with everything in him."

He could see the glimmer of tears in her eyes. "You think so?" she whispered.

"I know so. I think you already understand about the special bond between those of us who, as you put it, are willing to do a dangerous job to keep our families and our country safe. We train as a team, knowing every member's contribution is vital. That's why we go back—to not let our buddies down. To continue keeping the ones we love safe. We know they have other support. Our buddies have only us."

"I didn't have other support," she said quietly, looking away from him.

Fully committed now, he put out his hand and gently turned her chin back to face him. "Ross knew his family would be there for you. But he also saw, like I do, that you had an even more powerful resource. You yourself. Just as he saw your beauty and talent from the first, he saw your strength. Even if you didn't see it. I'm not saying that it wasn't hard, that sometimes you didn't think you'd make it through. But you did. And you're stronger now than you've ever been."

He held his breath, willing her to believe him. Knowing if she didn't, he had probably just destroyed any chance for them to end up together.

After a long moment which had him cursing himself for plowing ahead and probably ruining everything, she brought a hand up to curl her fingers around his. "Maybe," she admitted at last. "I sure didn't see it, not back then. I am stronger now, I know."

She glanced over at Katie, as if to confirm the girl was still peacefully sleeping—"Strong enough, in fact, that I talked to my mother a few days ago. Told her I want to bring Katie to visit, but not if she's going to ignore my suggestions and countermand my authority. I told her I want her to stop buying expensive gifts outside of Christmas and birthdays, that just having her spend time with Katie is gift enough. And that my daughter is too young to spend weeks away from me now, but we can revisit that when she's older. It felt . . . liberating to stand up to my mother!" She blew out a breath. "Like I'm finally a real grown-up."

"You did defy her before, when you got married in the teeth of her opposition."

"That was more like running away—I just left with Ross without ever confronting her. I never confronted her, growing up. If she pushed me to do something I didn't want, I'd avoid it if I could, but if I couldn't avoid, I just went along. This really was the first time I've ever made a stand. I would have come round to the necessity of doing it eventually, probably, but thanks for pointing the way."

"So you feel comfortable about the outcome?"

"Absolutely. Mother had almost nothing to say—a true rarity, believe me! Resolving that situation relieved a lot of anxiety."

"Then I'm glad you did it. Bravo."

"Thank you for inspiring me. And . . . for what you just said about the Corps. It makes me feel . . . better."

He leaned over to kiss her fingers. "Praise heaven. I was half-afraid you would slug me for being presumptuous enough to believe I could understand what you've been through."

"Even though I never bothered to try to understand what you've been through? You were injured, too, weren't you?"

Encouraged that she was asking about that previously taboo part of his life, he nodded. "Medivacked out of a firefight. Lost almost every man in my squad. Spent seven months in hospitals and rehab. I could have stayed in the Corps, but they would have assigned me to a desk job. I already felt bad enough about leaving my buddies out there on that hill to die."

"Oh my gosh! I had no idea. But—surely you know you did everything you could."

"My head does. My heart doesn't always believe that."

"Funny thing about hearts. Not to mix metaphors too much, but they can have a mind of their own."

Not until he knew she'd accepted all that he was without pushing him away did he realize that holding back about that vital part of his life had been the last thing that had kept him from falling for her completely.

His heart had a mind of its own for sure, and it was committing itself to her, completely.

Could he woo her into giving hers to him as well?

She nodded to acknowledge his praise. "Now—from the theoretical back to the practical. We were talking about the countertops, weren't we? Since you can't get away to look at them in person, should I text pictures of the ones I'm considering?"

Better to get back to the practical, before he got carried away and went down on one knee here and now. "I think by now we've established that I trust your vision. Whatever you pick will work fine."

"Once countertops are delivered and installed, and you finish up shiplap on the walls, we'll be really close to having everything done. I still have to make and install the rest of the lanterns for the walls and hallway, assemble the branding-iron chandelier, and get the chairs, barstools and tables done and transported."

"I'm just waiting on the plumber to deliver and install the shower unit. Once that's in, I'm ready to move in and finish the rest of it around me."

"Are you sure? I haven't yet looked around for those iron bedframes."

"I'm a Marine," he said, beyond delighted that he didn't have to tiptoe anymore around admitting who he was. "I'm used to sleeping on the ground. A rock-free floor is a luxury."

"A bed is better still."

*With her in it.* He couldn't help swinging his gaze to hers. Or recognizing the moment when she realized the sensual implications of that seemingly innocent remark.

He could tell that she, too, was envisioning of the two of them entwined on his bed in the aftermath of making love, gazing out at the starlit Texas night. Hungering for it, almost able to taste it, he found himself leaning toward her. As she leaned toward him.

The kiss was soft, sweet—and this time, Abby didn't draw away. Which was good, because he wasn't sure he could have. His hand rising up to grasp her chin, he brushed his lips back and forth against hers, touched his tongue to the seam at the corners of her mouth. And felt a thrill as strong as the surge of arousal when she opened for him.

Fireworks of delight and desire went off in his brain and exploded all over his body as he deepened the kiss. Another thrill went through him as *her* hand came up to clutch his shoulder and hold him in place.

For long, ecstatic minutes he explored the depths of her mouth, sampling, nibbling, tasting, reveling in the interplay of her tongue with his. By the time she pulled away, her lips rosy from his kiss, her face flushed and her eyes smoky, he was glad of the awkward arrangement of them kissing while seated in two separate, unyieldingly hard, wooden chairs.

Craving the warmth and softness of his body against hers, but for that separation, he might not have been able to keep himself from unbuttoning her blouse to press kisses down her throat, and lower. Keep his hands from caressing down her curves, rubbing his thumbs over her breasts to feel her nipples harden.

All of which might have scared her into retreating from him, instead of sinking slowly back into her chair, still a willing participant in those wondrous kisses.

"Don't apologize," she murmured, holding up a hand. "I shouldn't have kissed you back. I really don't mean to be a tease. It's just—it was such a wondrous day from beginning to end! Thank you again for it—for me and Katie. For telling me about the Corps and what you went through. And for that."

She touched his still-tingling lips with her fingertip. "I didn't think it would be possible for me to kiss someone without feeling awkward and guilty afterward. You've just proved that's not true. Because I feel . . . delighted. Thanks for helping me feel comfortable about being a woman again."

Beyond gratified, he said, "My pleasure, believe me. Anytime you're ready to . . . expand your repertoire, let me know."

She gave him a teasing little smile he could almost call . . . enticing. "I'll be sure to. Now, I'd better get my sleepy girl home. Before I'm even more indiscreet."

"Can't have that." *Yet, anyway.* Desire still pulsed in him, his insistent body not as patient as his brain needed it to be.

Firmly, he suppressed his need. Abby had just shown

him how much she was worth waiting for. If he was going to try to persuade his no-strings-attached girl to go further, he was going to have to step slowly and carefully. Because the only steps he wanted now led to permanent and forever.

"Let's get your gear, and I'll carry Katie to the truck for you."

"You'll have to be stealthy. I don't want her to wake up. She wants to stay here forever. Failing that, she's already asked if I could build Moondust a stall in my workshop."

Grant smiled as Abby packed up the few things she'd brought for their dinner, then carefully gathered the sleeping girl in his arms.

Neither spoke as they walked to her truck—letting moonlight and the magic of the beautiful evening shimmer between like the memory of those sweet, stirring kisses. As Grant settled the sleeping child into her seat and buckled her in, he thought the day couldn't have had a more perfect ending.

Unless Abby were staying here to spend the night with him.

Katie secured, he walked around to the driver's side while Abby climbed up into her truck.

"Thanks, partner. This cabin is going to be a dream come true." *So would she, if he could win her.*

"I sure hope so. I want it to be for you."

He took her hand, kissed it and placed it on the steering wheel. "Drive safe."

"Night, Grant."

He stood and watched as she drove away, a bubble of joy filling him. He couldn't remember ever feeling so . . . content, so at peace and at one with the land, certain he was in the right place—with the right person. He walked back to the cabin, intending to shut off the lights and lock up, then stopped.

Looking out across the valley, the river a moonlit silver line in the distance below, he wanted to linger and savor the wonder. Shutting off the lights, guided by moonlight, he walked back to his truck and pulled out the blankets he always kept there in case of an emergency and carried them back to the porch.

He'd sleep here tonight. And dream of sleeping here one day with Abby wrapped in his arms.

# Chapter Seventeen

A WEEK LATER, Abby loaded up her truck with design sketches, sample pieces of the supergood-deal quartz countertop she'd negotiated for the cabin, pics she'd taken of the two iron bedframes she'd found in one of her favorite resale shops on her way back from the stone yard in San Antonio, and one piece each of the linens, cookware, china and cutlery orders that had just been delivered. Marge was at the house with Katie, going over the week's worth of orders, and would take Katie back to her house for dinner when she finished. After Abby met Grant out at the cabin to show him the pictures and samples, she would continue into Whiskey River to join her daughter and friends.

She stopped by the mailbox before hopping into her truck and tossed the mail on the seat with her project folder and the samples. Although most of her business orders were placed directly online, sometimes clients would mail in a request. Maybe among the sales circulars and contribution pleas, there might be a few new orders. Smiling at the idea of seeing Grant again, she put the truck in gear.

She smiled all the way to the cabin. She'd initially feared

she would regret kissing him, once the magic of the moment faded—but she hadn't. For the first time since she lost her husband, being close to another man felt—right. Not that, like Marge had said, she was ready for a wedding bouquet and a ring, but maybe it *would* be nice to have a handsome, congenial companion of the male persuasion to talk with, share a glass wine with, go to a movie or out to dinner with. Kiss, hold hands with . . . and maybe later, when she felt ready, something more.

Those butterflies that seemed to be growing ever-bigger wings battered the sides of her stomach as she thought of his bedroom with the view into the valley. She was beginning to think it might not be impossible to envision a-few-strings-attached affair with a good friend. Once Grant was a former client, anyway.

Maybe . . . maybe even something more permanent.

Humming a tune as she turned the truck down the grass path leading to the cabin, she noted that his truck wasn't yet parked outside. Good. She'd grab her folders, samples and the mail and take it out to the front porch. Enjoy the peace and serenity as she sifted through it to see if there was anything worth reading.

After parking and carrying the stuff to the porch, she took a seat in the Adirondack chair she'd occupied the night he made them dinner after the trail ride. Smiling again, little shivers went through her as she remembered the kisses they'd shared. Oh, yes, she was hungry for more.

Most of the mail was ad circulars, but at the bottom was a larger legal envelope. She frowned as she saw the law office return address and Dallas postmark. *What in the world?*

Curious, she unfolded and read the letter. As she reached the end, the bottom dropped out of her stomach and all thought of samples, cabins and remodeling went straight out of her head.

SHE WASN'T SURE how long she paced the front porch—it seemed like forever—but it was probably only ten or fifteen minutes before she heard the sound of Grant's truck driving up.

*You will not cry*, she told herself as she waited for the motor to die, the truck door to close, and his footsteps to approach. *Take a deep breath. Stay calm. Be businesslike. Show him the samples, discuss what you need to, and head out. Then you can think about what to do about this.*

Though the concept of 'thinking' hardly penetrated through the maze of dread and anxiety imprisoning her.

Using every bit of willpower, she summoned up a smile as Grant rounded the corner and stepped onto the porch. "Sorry I'm late! Something about a cow stretching out a section of fence. Figured I'd better take a few minutes and repair it on the spot rather than leave it and chance having to chase her down later if she got through it before I could get back to it. So, what do you have to show me?"

She looked up, but before she could get out a word, his smile vanished. "Hell, Abby, what's happened? You look like you just stepped on your own grave!"

She went to speak and produced only a gasp. Realizing if she tried to open her mouth, she was going to fall apart, she silently handed him the letter.

Frowning, he read it over, then looked up at her. "Your parents are suing for guardianship of Katie on the basis of child endangerment? 'Lack of supervision and hazardous living conditions'? What the f—What's that about?"

"I should never have told Mother! You know I put up a gate in the workshop. I did it because last year, I was working on welding a project while Katie was at her worktable. Apparently she got curious about what I was doing and walked over without me noticing her approach. She got too close, got burned by some sparks from the welding torch. Horrified, I rushed her to the pediatrician. Thankfully, she only suffered a few first-degree burn spots. The doc told me to keep salve on it and watch the areas carefully, but that they would probably heal quickly, which they did. The incident scared me to death, though, so I put up the gate and put in a lockable cabinet to store anything poisonous or flammable. But as you'll see in the addendum"—she pointed it out—"it says 'the child has access to a work area which has the proven potential of having her suffer burns, cuts from broken glass and sharp tin, injury from half-finished pieces of raw iron and from chemicals used to strip and refinish wood. This parent often works with these items without having her child supervised by another adult.'"

"But that's bullshit! Katie doesn't have 'access.' You do have a gate and a cabinet to lock things up."

"The next addendum states the parent has 'variable income and might not be able to provide basic food, shelter and clothing. That plaintiff has on numerous occasions had to provide adequate clothing.'"

"She means those fancy dresses you didn't need anyway? Don't you think this is just your mother's way of upping the ante, trying to cow you into submission? Parental rights in law are very strong. Which I discovered when one of my troopers ran into a problem with his in-laws, who thought since he deployed to combat zones, they were better able to take care of their grandchildren than he was. Just the fact that the grandparents have more income and resources than the parent is not sufficient grounds for giving them custody. And no child protective service that investigated your workshop would believe Katie is in danger now."

Too frantic to remain motionless, she dropped the letter and resumed pacing. "Maybe it is just a threat. But you don't know my parents. They are very well-connected. They know every judge and politician in the state. All the high-powered lawyers. Even if they don't think they could win, they know going to court to contest the case would be tremendously expensive. Mother knows I can't afford it."

"You're not just going to give in, are you?" he asked, sounding enraged on her behalf.

She had to fight to stop the trembling in her lips long enough to reply. "I don't know what I'm going to do. Except that it would kill me to lose Katie." And then she couldn't hold it back any longer—the fear and anger and agonizing sense of helplessness. Putting her face in her hands, she sobbed.

"Ah, hell, Abby!" Grant stepped over and drew her against him, wrapping his arms around her while she wept.

After a few minutes, she pulled herself together and pushed away. "Sorry. I haven't given you any samples and I've left you with a soggy shirt."

"To hell with the samples. Abby, you don't need to capitulate. Fight back! First, any guardianship hearing would have to take place locally—not in Dallas where your parents know everyone. Marge and Jillee would testify to the care and supervision Katie has."

"She does come into the workshop with me."

"But you have the hazardous stuff secured."

"I guess I could take out a loan to pay for a lawyer." Then she remembered, and tears threated again. "Except I can't. That was the reason my business started the way it did. After they saw how I'd redone my house, and done some items on commission, friends and clients encouraged me to turn refurbishing into a business. I applied at the bank downtown for a small business loan. They turned me down flat. I had no credit history, no savings, I live in a rented house, and I didn't have any collateral. How could I get the funds I would need to fight my parents in court?"

Grant was silent for a minute, as if he were searching for an answer to that question she'd not been able to discover. Then he said quietly, "Marry me, Abby."

Eyes going wide with shock, she gazed up at him while he continued. "You know I care about you and Katie. You'd be much less vulnerable to anything your parents charge if you were married. You'd have more income, more support. There'd be two live-in adults to supervise Katie. And you'd be a McAllister—not Dallas royalty, maybe, but a member of one of the original pioneer families in this part of Texas. The only viable argument in your mother's case is the threat to Katie's safety. Negate that, and no judge in the world would agree to hand over custody. And the case would be tried here. I promise you, no judge for six counties around would believe a McAllister would neglect his child. I wouldn't have to risk the Triple A as collateral to pay a lawyer; I own a condo in San Antonio. I can mortgage that to raise the funds. Marry me, Abby. Let me help you end this for good."

Relief, anguish, fear, doubt and uncertainty buffeted her. "How could I let you do that?"

"I know asking you now is way too soon, way too fast. But honestly, I have been thinking about a future between us for a while now. Something more intimate and lasting than friends. Haven't . . . haven't you considered it too?"

"I've only just started to," she admitted.

"Look, if things didn't work out, we could always get divorced later. But in the meantime, Katie would be protected—from shenanigans like *that*," he ended, contempt in his voice as he pointed at the letter.

Swallowing the tears that threatened, she said, "I can't tell you how much I appreciate your offer, and I know we could get an easy divorce later. But . . . marriage still means something to me. Something a lot more than a casual, temporary arrangement. Just like I can't be casual about . . . sleeping with you. It's helped so much, just having someone to talk this over with."

"Yeah, I've been a big help," he retorted. "I'm the one who advised you to confront your mother, who answered with this shit. So I feel this whole debacle is at least partly my fault. Let me help you fix it. I'll ask Brice to ask his law enforcement contacts who would be the best judge to hear the case, if it comes to that. The McAllister name still means something around here."

Grant, willing to sacrifice his freedom to help her. Even though it was way too soon for him to make a commitment too. If he were fierce enough a friend to be willing to go that far to protect her and Katie, she could grow a backbone.

"You might be right, though. This letter might just be Mother's way of upping the ante. To scare me into capitulating and letting her do what she wants with Katie. So though I can't thank you enough for your offer, I think first I should go confront her in person. Find out whether she's truly ready to fight this out in court. She's never believed me capable of taking care of myself or standing up to her. With good reason. Yes, I defied her to marry Ross, but I had him to support me. Now she thinks I have no one."

Grant took her hand and kissed it. "She's wrong. You have me."

She nodded. *Damn, you will not cry again.* After sucking in a deep, calming breath, she said, "I'll talk to Marge and ask her to keep Katie for a day or so. Then call Mother and arrange to meet her in Dallas. If she stands firm and it does comes to a court trial, I . . . I will consider your offer then."

"I wish I could go with you. But you can do this, Abby."

"For Katie, I can do anything."

"Before you go to Dallas, let me talk to Brice and let him know what's going on. And give you his cell number. There's no harm having a Texas Ranger ready to back you up if things get ugly with your mother."

"But he doesn't even know me!"

"He knows me. If I vouch for you, that'll be good enough for Brice."

"The guy with the Ranger star, riding to the rescue? Thanks, Grant. For everything. I'll just leave these samples with you. You can let me know if any of them don't suit you. Going out of town will mean a delay in finishing up the cabin, though. I'm sorry."

He waved a dismissive hand. "Hang the delay. Nothing

is more important than Katie. Text me your plans, won't you? I'll talk to Brice and then send you his phone number. Let me know if there's anything else I can do."

"After offering to sacrifice yourself on the altar of marriage and volunteering your Ranger brother to protect me? You've done quite a lot already. Thanks, Grant."

She was about to turn to go when he stepped to her again. Pulling her back into his arms in a bone-crushing hug, he kissed her.

This wasn't a tentative, sweet exploration, but a hard, deep, mark of possession that left her senses reeling—and hungry for more.

"Don't ever doubt how much I want you," he said as he released her.

All she wanted that moment was to kiss him back. But luring him into having sex and losing herself in the euphoria of release would only delay having to solve the problem she faced. And unlike the kisses they'd shared, it might well leave her with regrets.

"I'd better go. I have to get planning."

He touched a finger to her nose. "Chin up. Be fierce, like I know you can be. Just think of how you bargained that discount owner down to nothing to get those furnishings. You'll be even more of a lioness to safeguard your daughter."

"Right. Roar," she said weakly, and then more loudly, "ROAR!"

"That's the spirit. Good luck. And let me know how

things go."

"Will do."

Setting her jaw, Abby picked up the letter and headed back to her truck.

# Chapter Eighteen

THREE DAYS LATER, Abby pulled into the exclusive residential community in Richmond Heights and punched the access code into the security gate keypad. After it slowly opened, she drove her truck through and down the spacious lanes of large mansions that made up her parents' neighborhood.

For the last two days, she'd been too nervous to eat. She wanted to believe Grant—that her mother's case was weak, that the letter from the lawyer—probably a family friend doing them a favor—was just meant to scare her into letting Mother control her—and Katie—as she always had.

Her feelings about Grant were a mixed-up mishmash that only intensified the anxiety swirling in her gut. Lingering shock as well as gratitude for his offer. A sneaky, cowardly urge to marry him immediately and let him and his Texas Ranger brother fight this battle. A deep reservoir of tenderness that whispered maybe marrying him was what she really wanted anyway.

But she'd worked too hard for too long to haul herself up from despair and stand on her own two feet. She might need

Grant and his Ranger brother eventually, and if she had to call on them in order to keep her daughter, she would.

But this first round was hers to fight. Before she could even think about the possibility of a future with Grant, she had to settle with her mother.

She pulled up in front of the large, brick mansion with its colonnade of tall, white Doric pillars that always made her think of Tara in *Gone With the Wind*. She certainly always pictured her mother as Scarlett O'Hara, a beauty who thought herself the reigning belle of three counties.

A belle used to manipulating people and getting what she wanted. Well, not when it came to Katie.

Normally, Abby dressed in old jeans, boots and a work shirt, but for the meeting today, she'd chosen a cotton sundress that flattered her figure and espadrille lace-up sandals. She'd styled her hair and actually applied some of the makeup she almost never wore. She wouldn't let Mother start on her with the usual immediate diatribe about how ill-kempt she looked.

She still had a house key, but this time, she knocked on the front door. Lucia, the family's longtime maid, opened it a few minutes later. Her surprise turning to a smile, she exclaimed, "Señorita Abby! How pretty you look! Señora Richardson is waiting in the sunroom."

Abby knew the way, of course, but she let the maid usher her in. Mother enjoyed the ceremony of having callers introduced and was always annoyed when Abby just slipped

JULIA JUSTISS

into the house she'd once lived in. One more concession to reserve all her energy for the important confrontation to come.

"Señorita Abby to see you, ma'am," the maid said, curtseying.

"Ah, Abby," her mother said, giving her a regal nod toward a seat on the sofa. "Bring us coffee, please, Lucia."

After the maid exited, Abby said, "Your letter accomplished what you intended. It brought me up here."

"Prepared to be reasonable, I hope."

"If by 'reasonable,' you mean prepared to give up my daughter, then no. Why do you even want her? A little girl requires a lot of time, Mother. Time you wouldn't be able to spend golfing, playing bridge, meeting friends for lunch, attending fashion shows and gallery openings."

"There's always that wonderful thing called an 'au pair,' darling."

"Face it, Mother, you see Katie as just another pretty little girl you could dress up and turn into a model like Ashley. Like you failed to do with me. If she were chubby or ugly, you wouldn't want anything to do with her."

Her mother shrugged. "What would I do with an ugly child? I've already suffered through raising a homely one. Though, I admit, you eventually turned out better than I'd hoped. Decently dressed and made up like you are today, you are quite presentable."

"Thank you," Abby said drily. But for the first time, her

mother's barb didn't sting quite so much. That must be progress, she thought, her nervousness easing a little.

Hostilities ceased for a few minutes as Lucia brought in and poured them coffee. After the maid retreated and they'd both taken several sips, anxious to get this fight over and done with, Abby said, "Let's get back to the point of this visit. You can force a custody battle. But you can't win it."

"Are you so sure? Those burn scars on Katie's forearm are real. You still work in that workshop with sharp metal and broken glass and all sorts of toxic cleaners and solvents, don't you? And you still take Katie out there with you while you do it, your attention on your work, not on her?"

"I have safeguards in place now," she countered, prepared to strike back at her mother's strongest argument. "What occurred last year was an accident. It won't happen again."

"So *you* say. A judge concerned for her welfare might see it differently. How would you pay for a trial anyway? That pitiful little shop you run reselling bits and pieces of junk can't bring in much income. Lawyers are expensive and a custody trial could be long."

The image of Grant's angry face, backing her up with his incredible offer, helped her push away that worry. "Maybe. But Katie is safe, she loves her mommy and wants to live with her. She's old enough for a judge to take that into account."

"Okay, let's say we go to court and I lose. What about

the publicity of being on trial for being a negligent mother? I imagine most of your clients are young women with limited means. When images of a child with a burned arm go viral on social media, you think they would continue to be willing to spend their few precious dollars buying goods from a woman accused of neglecting her child?"

For an instant, the possibility of her mother exploiting social media to ruin her business shocked her into silence. But only for an instant.

"I'm impressed you even know about the power of online media, but I'm not worried. Those who know me, know the truth. Maybe business would slow for a while, but there will always be more customers, once the furor died down. I'd still have Katie and I can wait it out. Because you *will* lose. I promise you that."

She stared at her mother, hoping she looked not defiant, but full of implacable resolve.

"I wouldn't be so sure," her mother answered, but in the face of Abby's resolution, her arrogantly confident demeanor was slipping a bit.

"Speaking of sure, why are you even doing this? Of course, I know Katie is darling, but that isn't the reason you want her, is it? You've ignored me for years. Why this attempt at grabbing my daughter, now?"

Suddenly a possible explanation occurred to her. "Is all this because Ashley moved to New York six months ago and you don't have her company anymore? You can't be . . .

you're not . . . *lonely*, are you?"

"Don't be ridiculous," her mother scoffed. "I have more friends than you'll ever make in the dusty backwater you've chosen to rusticate in." But her lacquered nails fiddled with the edge of her napkin and she didn't meet Abby's eye.

Abby thought back to her recent weekends visits. Now that she considered it, there had been few phone calls, no one who stopped by to chat. She wasn't sure her mother really did have friends—other than the social acquaintances she met for lunch and shopping.

Something else struck her then, something she hadn't looked at closely before. "Now that I think of it, yours is the only signature on the papers. Does Father even know about this?"

Her mother's fingers grew more restless. "He's been busy. I did . . . mention it."

"Rundell, Martin and Evers," Abby named the law firm that had sent the letter. "Rob Rundell is the guy who courted you before you married Father, isn't he? So you talked him into having his office make up the paperwork. Did he think you would really go through with filing a case?"

"I didn't think we'd have to!" her mother burst out. "All right, your father doesn't know. Life has been . . . emptier since Ashley moved. We used to talk every day, have lunch four or five times a week. But her career is going so fabulously well in New York, she's incredibly busy. We don't . . . talk like we used to, and your father is always so occupied with his business contacts. I never noticed just how much until Ashley left. He no longer seems to have . . . time for me. To be honest, I think he has a mistress."

What a blow that admission must be, Abby thought, shocked. "I'm sorry."

"'Sorry?'" her mother spat out angrily. "You don't know what it's like—how could you? To go from being courted and flattered and waited on to being . . . almost ignored." She gave a bitter laugh. "Yes, I met with Rob and talked him into having his office draw up the papers for me. Once, I'd only have to bat my eyelashes at him to get him to do whatever I asked. This time, he told me in honor of our long friendship, he'd give me a discounted price for his office's services. A *discount*! After Ashley left, I started remembering how full life was when she was little. The fun of taking her to modeling sessions and pageants. The excitement, the glamour. Katie is just as pretty as Ashley was, maybe even prettier. I thought how wonderful it would be to have that back again."

Abby felt what she'd never imagined she could feel for her beautiful, regal, controlling mother. Sadness. "We can't go back and relive the past, Mother. We have to move forward into the future. As I know better than anyone."

"What future?" she scoffed. "You'd have me come to that little hick town, put on old jeans like the ones you live in, forget about makeup, put my hair up in a bun and sit in dust making mud pies? I can't do that."

"No, I wouldn't. Though you might consider visiting the Hill Country again—it really is beautiful, like a slice of heaven. It boasts some excellent wineries. We could go riding—Katie loves it. Or I could bring Katie to Dallas and you could take her to the zoo, the stockyards in Fort Worth, Children's Night at the Dallas Museum of Fine Arts. Read books with her. Yes, and play dress-up and play with makeup. But let her be a little girl. She'll grow up soon enough. Let me be her mommy. And let yourself be her mimi."

When her mother said nothing, she continued, "It's a fair offer, Mother. The only one I'm prepared to make, so don't think you can try to bargain or coerce me. Take it, let the past be the past, and let's move forward. Or you could go on with this court fight, trying to hang onto a fairy-tale vision of some vanished world, and lose everything. Make things too unpleasant, and after I win—and I will win—I might be forced to cut off all contact with you completely. I know we've had our differences, but I really don't want it to come to that."

And she didn't, Abby realized. As much as her mother had hurt and neglected her, bullied and ignored her—Gwenneth Richardson was still her mother, part of the past that had forged her into who she was today. She really would like to salvage the relationship—and move it in a new, better direction.

But whether or not that happened was now entirely up

to her mother.

She waited while her mother sipped her coffee, saying nothing. While the hands that held her mother's cup trembled.

Her mother saying nothing was already a battle won. She always had the last word. When she didn't rush to make a rebuttal, Abby felt more confident than ever that the whole guardianship business had been no more than a charade from the beginning, a threat designed to make Abby fall into line.

As she stared at her mother's averted face, she noticed the lines on her forehead, at the corners of her eyes and mouth that the makeup no longer masked. The slight sag of her chin, the veins in her hands that were now more prominent. Her mother was hardly over the hill, but she was no longer an outstandingly beautiful woman. Abby had always been so dazzled by her, until this moment, she hadn't looked closely enough to notice.

How terrifying growing old must be for a woman who had for her whole life defined her worth by her looks and her ability to use them to entice men and maneuver women. For the first time in her life, she felt sorry for her mother.

"We can work this out, Mother," she said softly, reaching out to touch her mother's hand. "I don't want to deprive you of the joy of having Katie in your life."

Her mother drew back her hand. "I'm quite capable of finding joy for myself."

That sounded more like her mother. So much for feeling

sympathetic.

Abby finished her coffee and set down the cup. "I'm heading home now. Call me after you've decided what you want to do. Maybe we can plan something for Katie's birthday next month."

She watched her mother warily, but the last-stand assault she half-expected didn't materialize. She couldn't follow through on the lawsuit threat without Abby's father's support, and she knew it.

With a rising sense of euphoria, Abby stood and picked up her purse.

"Goodbye, Mother. I'll expect to hear from you soon."

"You'll hear from me, all right. Yes, go on back to your dusty little 'slice of heaven.'"

Abby smiled. Her mother might be cowed, but she wasn't going to let Abby leave without delivering one last jab.

"It is heaven. You should spend enough time there to see for yourself."

She walked out and back to her truck, having all she could do not to kick her heels and whoop with joy. She'd stood up to her mother, called her bluff—and won.

Grant would say she'd become a pretty damn good poker player.

Oh, my. Grant. What was she going to do about him?

BACK IN WHISKEY River, dusty, gritty, and grimy, Grant finished mowing the meadow and drove the tractor back to the Scott barn. Not until he put all the equipment away and wiped the sweat from his face did he pull out his cell phone.

Which had a text from Abby. Sucking in a nervous breath, he thumbed open the phone and read it.

*I'm pretty sure you were right and it was a bluff. Don't think M will go through with filing papers. Offered her a compromise. Heading home. Will tell you more when I get back.*

Grant read the message over again, relieved for Abby, but not so sure how he felt. Despite the apparent success of her trip, his offer to marry her was still on the table.

Would she take him up on it?

She'd faced dark times, too, just as dark as his. She'd come through, reinvented herself and flourished. She'd already helped him through the hurdle of his reduced cash flow. Normally, a man took care of his woman—but this woman seemed willing to take care of those she cared about too. Despite a lifetime of being belittled, dominated and diminished, she'd found the courage to stand up and fight for what she loved. Her love and loyalty to her child as unshakeable as the loyalty she'd demonstrated to her late husband.

Yes, this was a woman he could trust with his heart, for joy in good times, for support in times of trial. Not until after he'd asked her to marry him had he realized just how much he wanted to make her his wife.

Not just to help her keep Katie. So he could love and cherish them both. For the rest of their lives.

But she said she wouldn't consider marrying him unless it was absolutely necessary in order to keep from losing Katie. Now that it appeared it wouldn't be necessary, would she distance herself from him? After their unexpected circumstances had prompted him to pressure her by going too far, too fast, too soon?

Now that he'd become absolutely convinced he loved her and wanted her forever, he wouldn't entertain the thought of losing her. No matter how much it hurt to wait, no matter how long it took to win her, he would do it.

He couldn't see any other way forward. Like that greenhorn rider who hadn't lasted a second on his first bronc, he was already head over heels.

After wiping off his grubby fingers, he texted her back, telling her he'd be waiting for her at the cabin. Saying a prayer for luck, he headed for the house to clean up.

A FEW HOURS later, while he paced the cabin's front porch, he heard the sound of Abby's truck approaching. Telling himself to stay calm, he waited, holding in his hand the "welcome back" glass of wine he'd poured for her.

He wished he dared kiss her, but not knowing where things stood, as she rounded the corner, he held out the wine instead. "I imagine you need this."

"Thank you!" she exclaimed, accepting the glass and taking a long swallow Sitting down in the chair he motioned her to, she said, "Looks like you've lucked out. You won't have to make that eleventh-hour sacrifice and marry me after all."

Leaving that remark to deal with later, he said, "Tell me everything."

For the next ten minutes, she did, relaying the gist of the conversation with her mother and its successful conclusion.

"Bravo, Abby. I'm thrilled that you're on the road to reconciling with your mother, on your terms. She might be a pain in the ass, but she's still your flesh and blood. It's not good to have dissension in the family."

"Thank for you for helping me charter the way to get there."

He paused, taking a sip of his own wine before saying, "But what if I don't think marrying you is a 'sacrifice'? What if I've come to believe it would be the smartest thing I ever did? Not immediately, of course. I know it's too soon for you to decide—now. But you do like me. You are attracted to me. And you said you were considering something . . . more."

She looked distressed, making him regret bringing this up. But they'd both said they wanted honesty. And he needed to know how she felt.

"I do like you, and I am attracted to you, I don't deny it. I'm . . . tempted. But . . ."

"But?" he prompted.

"After I learned about Ross's death, I was almost . . . cat-
atonic. I don't remember much about the first few months.
Marge and Ross's mother, Helen, arriving at base housing,
coaxing me to come to Whiskey River with them. Sleeping
or sitting in the dark in his old room at his mother's, hardly
ever leaving the house. Lost in a cataclysm of grief. My whole
world had revolved around Ross, the one person who'd ever
seemed to find me fun and pretty and who valued the things
I crafted."

She paused, and Grant waited for her to continue, trying
not to let her words chip away at the hopes he'd begun
cherishing. "Not until I felt my baby move, and realized I
was now responsible for another life, was I able to begin
pulling myself together. Ross might be gone, but he'd left me
his daughter. I needed to take better care of myself to give
her the best start in life. And I needed to figure out how to
earn a living to give us both the chance for a better life. And
I have. It was long and difficult, but I've made an independent life for us. I just don't know if I have it in me to care that
much for anyone again and be able to recover if I suffered
another loss. And it's not just that. By being unsure, I'd be
putting Katie at risk too."

"Put Katie at risk? You know I'd never let anything happen to her!"

"You wouldn't *want* to hurt her. But—what if I finally
decide I can't offer anything more than friendship? When I

said goodbye to Katie after I took her to Marge's, she . . . she asked me if you were going to be her daddy. She said that Sissie gets to see her daddy on weekends, and Meghan's daddy lives with her when he's not working, but she's never had a daddy of her own, and she thinks you would be 'the bestest daddy ever.' I think we need to keep our distance. So Katie doesn't get even more attached to you. I don't want to break her heart. I don't want to break yours, either. I think I should only see you as much as is necessary for me to complete the cabin."

Even though he'd told himself not to expect her to accept his proposal, learning that she didn't just want more time, she wanted a lot more distance, hurt more than he could have imagined.

But pressing her, arguing, wasn't going to convince her, and it could only drive her further away. So he swallowed the words, despite how much he wanted to plead for her to give them more of a chance.

Instead, he nodded. "Okay. I won't press you and I'm willing to keep my distance to protect Katie, if that's what you want. But I'm not going to give up on us. I'll be here, anytime you want to talk. Anytime you want to see me. Until you are sure as I am, one way or the other."

"I'm sorry, Grant. I wish I could give you a better answer."

"Don't be sorry. Even if you decide I'm not what you want, I'll never be sorry for meeting you, getting to know you. Falling in love with you."

"Now you're making me feel guilty. You've been so good to us, so—"

"I don't want you feeling guilty," he interrupted, wiping a tear from the corner of her eye. "And I don't want your gratitude. I want you joyful. I want you to look at me the same way you look at Katie. With a love that's pure, absolute and undimmed by any doubt. Love me like you trust I'll be here for you, forever."

"You can't promise that! No one can."

"Sure, I could get caught in a rockslide or hit by a lightning bolt or have a horse kick me in the head. There are no absolute guarantees in life. But even if something happened later, we'd have the time together now. You're a strong woman, Abby—even you know that now. You've shown you're able to weather whatever might happen. And loving me wouldn't threaten the independence you've work so hard to build. Loving doesn't require ceding control over your life, or becoming weak or dependent. It means sharing your strengths and bolstering each other's weaknesses. You'll always be the strong, independent woman you've made yourself. I'm proud of your business and all you've accomplished and would encourage you to keep expanding it. But you could have *us* too. Or you can walk away."

"If I have to choose right now, I have to walk away."

"I'm not making you choose. Just asking you not to give up on the idea, either." He gave her a smile, knowing it looked forced. "In any event, we still need to work together to finish up the cabin."

Deciding in that instant, knowing he needed to get away and have space to clear his head and ease the pain in his heart, he said, "I have to go to San Antonio next week. See some of my VA clients, check about supplies for that electric boundary fence. I told Duncan about your ideas for using the Scott barn and have his tentative approval to contact the local Ys and the MWR units on the different bases. As for the cabin, if you'll finish up the design work, I'll complete any of the heavier stuff when I get back."

Tears in her eyes again, she whispered, "Thanks for being so understanding. You're a wonderful guy, and I—"

"Don't," he interrupted, having had about as much emotional turmoil as he could take at the moment. "Just . . . don't. Please, Abby."

"Okay," she said in a small voice. "It's getting late. I'd better be going. I texted Marge that I was back in Whiskey River. Katie will be expecting me."

He'd have to let her walk away, even though it was the very last thing he wanted. Let her walk away and hope she'd decide to come back.

"Have a good week, Abby," he said, rising to take her wineglass. "I'll text you when I get back from San Antonio, see how things are going with the cabin."

"Okay. Thanks again—for everything."

He'd hoped he'd be kissing her again—not verbally shaking her hand goodbye. Gritting his teeth against the pain and frustration, he made himself remain on the porch while she walked back to her truck.

He blew out a breath as he listened to her driving away. Had leveling with her about the way he felt been the right choice? He might have scared her, pushed her away for good.

But it wasn't his declaration, it was her indecision about them and the possibility of hurting Katie that made her push him away.

He could appreciate her concern for her daughter. That darling little girl who wanted him to be her "bestest daddy ever." Warmth filling his heart, he acknowledged how much he'd like that too. Along with becoming Abby's bestest lover, for all her life.

But Abby would have to decide that was what *she* wanted.

And if she didn't choose him, somehow, he was going to have to learn to live with it.

# Chapter Nineteen

F OR THE WEEK that Grant was in San Antonio, Abby tried to keep herself so busy she didn't have time to think—or feel. With the usual abundance of orders for teacup lamps and several of her other favorite items coming in, plus doing the finishing touches on Grant's dining chairs and island barstools, painting the buffet and table legs, and completing the various light fixtures, she certainly had enough to occupy her.

But somehow, in the late evenings after she put Katie to bed, she couldn't quite keep thoughts of him from invading her mind. She'd find herself smiling, recalling his rope tricks. Appreciating his calm expertise as he helped her craft items at the cabin. Enjoying the way he delighted and entertained Katie.

Remembering the deep hunger he aroused with his kisses.

He'd flat-out assured her that he was proud of her business and would encourage her to continue building it, so she didn't need to fear choosing him would compromise the work she loved so much.

But was she wrong to fear her independence would be threatened if she gave herself up to loving again? To fear she wouldn't be strong enough to bear a second blow of loss, should something happen to him?

She'd missed him—even as busy as she'd kept herself. And when she contemplated what her life would be if she excluded him from it once the cabin was finished, all she could see was a yawning chasm of endless gray days without the sunshine of his presence, the delight of his laughter, the sensual fulfillment promised by his kisses.

Her memories had also been tinged with guilt. Though she certainly hadn't wanted to, she knew she'd hurt him.

He'd be back in Whiskey River soon. Did she really want to maintain a civil distance, treating him as just another client—until he wasn't even a client? Could she do it?

While she dithered, trying to decide on the right answer—one that would allow her to go forward confidently, without this gaping hole that seemed to have opened up in her chest, she increasingly heard whispering in her ear. A little voice that said, "Grow up. You've taken responsibility for your child, built a career, finally faced down your mother. Once and for all, let go of the rest of your childhood hurts and fully become the woman you are capable of being."

It had been different when Ross was in the Marines. There'd always been the chance of losing him—but Grant would not be deploying to a combat zone. Yes, some accident or illness might prematurely take him from her, but the odds of that were low.

Could she trust him to be true to her? That one she had no trouble answering—his integrity, from the moment she met him, had been unquestionable.

And he was right—she was stronger now than she'd been five years ago. She'd survived devastating loss—proving that she *could* survive it.

Was she, like that little voice kept insisting, letting all these old hurts keep her from fully embracing life now?

Grant had promised he'd wait for her to decide. But he shouldn't have to wait.

She needed to once and for all stop listening to her mother's voice in her head, the one that told her that with only a high school education, no job skills, no experience, no one would hire her to do anything. The voice that said she wasn't strong enough, wasn't good enough, wasn't brave enough to last six months on her own.

But she had lasted. With the help of Ross's family and her love for Katie, she'd pulled herself out of depression, harnessed her talents to make them a home and built a business. She needed to finally dismiss her little-girl fears and reach out to grasp a life that included not just love for her child and her work—but also love for one special man.

And if that happiness didn't last forever . . . she would survive.

Peace, acceptance, and a quiet sense of joy filled her heart. She was loved by a wonderful man. Why had it taken her so long to accept that blessing?

She didn't have much time before he returned to Whiskey River, and she'd wasted too much time already. She didn't intend to squander another minute before showing him that if he were still willing to take a chance on her, she was prepared to take that leap of faith with him.

And let the love she'd tried to evade and deny fill her heart and embrace him.

THREE DAYS LATER, Grant looked at his phone to find a text from Abby. Unconsciously, he put a hand on his chest, the constant ache he felt there warring with the fierce hope that had sustained him since he'd watched her walking away from the cabin.

He'd spent the week in San Antonio determined to leave her alone. He hadn't called or contacted her, had answered only her few brief texts about the cabin with equally brief replies.

He'd missed her desperately. How was it that, without him even noticing it, she'd managed to weave her way completely into the fabric of his life?

Chump. That's what he got for falling in love after promising himself to never depend again on anyone but family.

Chump.

But would he have missed knowing her? Missed having the chance of winning her?

No, he wouldn't.

And he hadn't entirely given up hope yet. When you first toss a lariat around a wild mustang, you don't always tighten it immediately. You can leave some slack in the rope, let the horse grow accustomed to the touch of it around his neck, so he doesn't fight as hard when you pull him in.

He hoped that sometime, she would be ready to come willingly. But in the end, if Abby found the past too hard to overcome, or if she just wasn't able to love him enough to surmount her fears, it wasn't going to work anyway.

Sighing, he thumbed the phone open and scrolled down to read the text she'd left.

*When are you returning to WR?*

*Tomorrow*, he replied.

After a few more texts back and forth, they agreed to meet at the cabin in the late afternoon, which would give him time to report back to Duncan and check on the cows and the condition of the meadows.

Time to try to steel himself to meet her and be friendly, cordial, but distant.

Could he keep the love and hope from shining in his eyes?

Maybe he should drop one of the heavy cast-iron pots she'd gotten him on his boot. The physical pain might be enough to distract him from the pain in his heart.

One way or another, tomorrow he'd drive back to Whiskey River, use all his willpower to restrain his response to her, and keep a tight rein on that stubborn sense of hope.

LATE THE NEXT afternoon, Grant drove toward the cabin. Despite telling himself not to expect anything more than a work session, he'd worn a nice pair of jeans, an ironed, collared shirt and his favorite boots for luck.

*You're going to laugh at yourself, you idiot, when you scuff up those shiny boots and get dirt all over your favorite shirt.*

Once again, though he'd thought he'd be early, Abby beat him there. As he approached and saw her truck parked beside the cabin, an ache of love, hope and longing resonated in his chest. No matter what happened this afternoon, at least he had this chance to see her.

He thought she might meet him on the porch, since she would doubtless have heard his truck driving up. No one appeared when he rounded the corner, so she must be working inside. She'd texted him that there were still a lot of finishing details she needed him to help with.

But when he walked inside, he had to stop short. Looking around, he marveled at what he saw. If there was still work to be done, he sure didn't know where.

The refinished sideboard beyond the dining table was a dull gleam of polished black, the wineglasses on the rake head holder sparkling. The matching black legs of the table contrasted with its polished wooden surface, along which a table runner in an open-weave, tan cotton ran down the center, topped with three black candleholders bearing beige candles. His gaze swept from the patterned rug peeking beneath the table and the white-finished chairs, to the beautiful blue, tan and ochre hues of the rug in front of the fireplace, anchored by its long chestnut rawhide couch. The two refinished chairs, their denim covering looking soft and inviting, posed nearby, all the seating finished with throw pillows in southwestern patterns in deep blues, tans, and dusty-ochre brick. Above the grouping, the Triple A brand chandelier dangled, its black trim echoing the buffet, the gas fireplace insert, and the window trim.

And the kitchen! Colorful knobs of fired clay in the homemade, upper cabinet doors picked up the tan, blue, and ochre colors in the rest of the room. Behind the chicken-wire doors, earth tone china was stacked. The dull gleam of concrete-gray quartz finished the counter, a subtle contrast to the whitewashed wooden cabinets, while the tin-roofing backsplash and backing for the island echoed the gray hues.

It looked like a photo shoot for a fancy interior design magazine. Beautiful. Yet entirely livable. A cowboy could feel comfortable, walking in at the end of a day dusty and tired from chasing down cows or mowing fields, to pour himself a beer, sink down onto the couch or in one of those over-stuffed chairs, prop his boots on the water-trough coffee table and relax in front of the fire.

"Do you like it?"

The sound of Abby's voice shocked him out of his trance. "Like it? It looks magnificent! I thought it would be wonderful, but this . . . this far exceeds anything I had imagined. Thank you, Abby."

Speaking of wonderful, *she* looked like every man's dream of the ideal woman. Rather than pulled up in a casual twist, her hair was braided and pinned into an intricate knot that made his fingers itch to unravel it, while wispy ringlets framed her face. A hint of shadow intensified the deep blue of her eyes, a dusting of powder gave a soft sheen to her face, and bright-red lipstick outlined lips that made his mouth water. Instead of her usual jeans, boots and work shirt, she wore a knit dress that clung to every curve in a deep blue that accentuated the blue of her eyes.

He wanted to scoop her up and devour her on the spot.

He had to look away as he fought to suppress the love flooding him and rein in his rampaging desire.

"In case you didn't notice," she was saying, "I didn't come dressed to work, since, actually, the cabin is finished. I wanted to surprise you."

"I am surprised," he said, finally managing to find his voice. "Impressed. Delighted."

*Though he'd be a lot less delighted if she ended this afternoon by announcing that since the cabin was finished, so were they.*

"I thought instead of working, we'd celebrate. First, I wanted to walk you through and show you all the rooms."

"Sure. I'm eager to admire all your hard work."

So, keeping a safe distance that allowed him to resist the hunger to put his hands on her, he followed her as she pointed out the features. The white-iron bedstead in the guest bedroom, with whitewashed storage side tables crafted from more wooden boxes with chicken-wire doors. The bathroom with its dark-painted vanity, bright-white farm sink, tin backsplash and black lantern sconces highlighting the gleam of the white shower unit. The row of black lantern sconces lighting the hallway that ran between the rooms of the new addition.

And finally, the master bedroom. A large, white-iron bedframe held pride of place, covered in bed linens in shades of tan and white with throw pillows of ochre, sage and deep blue, the bed facing the wall of windows with a magnificent vista of the hills, canyon and river beyond. The view framed by airy drapes of a pale, open-weave cotton that seemed to invite a person to gaze outside.

"It's wonderful, Abby," he whispered. "Everything I wanted and more."

"So you can envision lying there, looking out at the night sky spangled with stars?"

"Yes." *As I ache to be holding you in my arms.*

"Katie is having an overnight with Sissie at Marge's. So I don't have to be back . . . anytime soon."

Only then, as she walked over to it, did he pull his gaze away from the view to notice there was a champagne bottle in an ice bucket on the far-side end table. Opened and flanked by two glasses.

Trying to restrain his rampaging imagination, he stood stock-still, his brain incapable of producing speech, while Abby poured two glasses of the sparkling wine and brought them over to him.

"Here's to the successful completion of your cabin."

He touched his glass to hers and took a tiny sip. He didn't dare do much more than wet his lips, because he was already having a hard enough time controlling his hunger for her. He was pretty sure, under the influence of a little alcohol, his control would snap and he'd try to lure her onto that bed.

He tried to distract himself from that vision and ignore the potent scent of roses and woman that invaded his head as she stood beside him, sipping her wine. He tried to picture in his mind the meadows he had left to mow, calculate in his head the length of electric wire he'd need to run to finish the first length of border fencing, recall the price of beef that had been listed in this morning's daily Cattlemen's Association email.

Abby's hand on his arm made him jump. "Are you still sure you want me?" she whispered.

He took a gasping breath, not sure he could have heard correctly. "W-what?"

"Do you still want me?" she repeated, her voice louder.

Confused, he shook his head. "How could you doubt that? Yes, I want you. I'll always want you."

"Then I'm yours, cowboy. I thought we might . . . stay the night. Try out the bed. And that view under the stars."

Grant had been so afraid he'd lost her he could hardly believe he'd won her after all.

So instead of dumping his wineglass and yanking her into his arms, Grant said, "Are you sure? I'd never want you to do anything that made you feel uncomfortable. That left you with regrets. I don't do casual any more than you do. It's all-in or nothing."

"Then I'm ready to show you just how all-in I am." Taking both their wineglasses, she set them on the side table and walked back to him, holding out her arms.

Euphoria making his knees weak, he tipped up her chin to give her a long, sweet kiss. A "welcome back" kiss. An "I'm never leaving you again" kiss.

Then her tongue was tickling at the edge of his mouth, demanding entry. Before she could completely dismantle his ability to think, he broke the contact and stepped away.

"Then we better make it official. Wait right here. Don't move a muscle. Or have some more champagne, if you want. I'll be right back."

Feeling his chest might explode with happiness, Grant raced out to his truck, pulled a small box out of the glove compartment and loped back into the bedroom. Pulling

Abby, who was standing by the open window admiring the view, back to the bed, he motioned her to sit and then went down on one knee.

Holding out the box, he said, "Abby Rogers, will you marry me?"

Gazing at him tenderly, she took the box and opened it. "You got me a ring?"

He nodded. "While I was in San Antonio."

Laughing, she touched his lips with her finger. "You were that sure I would come to my senses and marry you after all, despite what I told you when we were here last time?"

"I wasn't sure at all. I just hoped you wouldn't leave me with a gaping hole in my heart for the rest of my life. I was playing poker, and betting on us. So—will you marry me?"

She leaned over to kiss him, wrapping her arms around his neck. "Yes, Grant McAllister, I will marry you. I decided I didn't want to live the rest of my life with a gaping hole in *my* heart. Or let old fears and insecurities keep me from reaching out to grasp the best, most beautiful happiness I could ever wish for."

After fitting his ring onto her finger, he sat next to her on the bed and pulled her into his arms, his passionate, hungry, desperate kisses proving just how much he wanted her.

Scooting back to recline against the pillows, Abby pulled him toward her. "We'll have to take it slow. I want you, but I'm a little . . . nervous. It's been a long time, and I don't have much experience."

"Why don't we wait a little longer, then? Unless you want some big fancy to-do, it won't take that long to put together a wedding. And then I can make love, here, to my forever bride."

Frowning, Abby shook her head. "No, I want to be close to you. Belong to you completely. Now."

He feathered another soft kiss across her lips. "I think it would be better to wait. I don't ever want you to have doubts or regret anything."

Her frown deepened. "I'm not doubtful, just nervous! I don't want to wait, Grant. I want all the joy that can be ours—today!"

When he said nothing, she said uncertainly, "Aren't you . . . impatient too?"

Unable to continue the charade any longer, he succumbed to the need to kiss those tempting lips again. Long and deep and possessively, so she would have no doubt how much he wanted her.

"Devil!" she said, batting his shoulder when he released her. "You were teasing me!"

He took her hands and kissed them. "The first time I set eyes on you, I thought you were the most beautiful, precious thing I'd ever seen. I've wanted to treasure you from that moment. I always will."

"Then start now," she murmured, and pulled him back onto the bed.

A WEEK LATER—ABBY had said she didn't want to wait a minute longer than necessary to make their union official— Grant stood with his brothers on the porch outside the cabin. They'd delayed only long enough to get a marriage license, find a day when Brice would be available, and coordinate the time with the minister at church.

In a few minutes, after a short ceremony, he'd be able to celebrate with his brothers, Abby's sister-in-law, friend Jillee, mother-in-law and the children in the most joyous event he could imagine. Something, when he'd come back to reclaim his family and his place in Whiskey River, he'd never expected.

"I'm not sure I want to visit the Triple A very often," Brice was saying. "This marrying thing seems to be contagious."

"He hopes he's immune," Grant said.

"Nobody's immune," Duncan said with a fond glance at Harrison, who was helping Sissie, Meghan and Katie tie flower garlands on their heads. "He just has to meet the right woman."

Then the minister stepped out onto the porch. "Gentlemen, ladies, the bride is ready."

Chest swelling with joy and anticipation, Grant walked with the others along the completed terrace from the front porch to the deck outside the master bedroom, which was

JULIA JUSTISS

decorated with more of the flowers the girls wore in their garlands. Billowy curtains of the same material Abby had hung inside framed the windows outside, making an arch topped with more flowers.

Under the arch, Abby waited, with a bouquet of white roses in her hands. Looking at her, ethereally beautiful with her blond hair swept up, her slender curves hugged by a knit dress of ice blue, made his toes curl with suppressed need and his heart effervescent with happiness.

Eyes never leaving her face, he walked over and took her hand. Repeated with her the traditional vows that would allow him to love, cherish and protect this vision of grace and brightness for the rest of his days.

As soon as the minister pronounced them man and wife, and he'd sealed their vows with a kiss, Katie bounded over. "Are you going to be my daddy now?"

"Yes, Princess, if you want me to be."

"Forever?"

Exchanging a tender glance with Abby, he nodded. "Forever and ever."

"Does that mean you'll finally take me fishing?"

Grant laughed. "You bet, Princess. Whenever we can."

"I still want to go fishing, but Sissie said after the wedding I could ask you for something I want almost as much."

"Moondust stabled in my barn?" Grant suggested.

Katie's eyes widened. "That would be awesome. But not that."

Abby linked her arm with his, her smile the light of his life. "What then, sweetheart?"

"I want a baby sister!"

While Abby colored, the guests laughed and Grant kissed Abby's hand. "We'll do our best, Princess. I can promise you that."

## The End

Want more? Check out Duncan and Harrison's story in *The Rancher*!

Join Tule Publishing's newsletter for more great reads and weekly deals!

If you enjoyed *The Cowboy,*
you'll love the next book in….

# The McAllister Brothers series

Book 1: *The Rancher*

Book 2: *The Cowboy*

Book 3: *The Ranger*
*Coming July 2021!*

*Available now at your favorite online retailer!*

# More books by Julia Justiss

*Scandal with the Rancher*

*A Texas Christmas Past*

*Available now at your favorite online retailer!*

# About the Author

After writing more than twenty-five novels and novellas set in the English Regency, award-winning historical author Julia Justiss expanded her focus to pen stories that take place on the frontier of the Texas Hill Country, near where she lives with her native-born Texas husband.

An avid reader who began jotting down plot ideas for Nancy Drew novels in her third grade spiral, Julia went on to write poetry and then speeches, sales promotion material and newsletters as a business journalist, before turning to fiction. Her awards include the Golden Heart for Regency from Romance Writers of America, The Golden Quill, and finals in Romantic Times Magazine's Best First Historical, the National Readers Choice, the Daphne du Maurier and All About Romance's Favorite Book of the Year.

Thank you for reading

# The Cowboy

If you enjoyed this book, you can find more from all our great authors at TulePublishing.com, or from your favorite online retailer.

TULE
PUBLISHING